UNDER THE GUN

Bullets began slamming into the iron skin of the sub—machine gun fire pelting the boat like a torrent of hailstones. Right now the big gun turrets of the destroyer would be swinging ominously onto the renegade U-boat.

In the control room, Tyler spoke into his intercom mike. "We're going down."

The ship was submerging, only the conning tower still exposed—the pinging of fire from MP-40s like a shooting gallery above the Control Room crew—and even without the scope to look through, Tyler knew his boat was dead smack in front of the destroyer at the moment the U-571 dipped under the waves. Bracing himself for a collision, half-expecting to feel the scrape of the warship's keel, Tyler waited, and waited. As did every man around him.

U-571

A NOVEL BY
MAX ALLAN COLLINS

BASED ON A MOTION PICTURE SCREENPLAY BY
JONATHAN MOSTOW AND **SAM MONTGOMERY** AND **DAVID AYER**

STORY BY
JONATHAN MOSTOW

AVON BOOKS
An Imprint of HarperCollins*Publishers*

AVON BOOKS, INC.
An Imprint of HarperCollins*Publishers*
10 East 53rd Street
New York, New York 10022-5299

First Avon Books Printing: April 2000

*This is for my writer buddy
Steve Mertz,
who runs deep, but rarely silent*

If you're going to set down the story of the submarines, you must first set down the story of the man inside the submarine—the man who fights it and nurses it and whose life is bound up with it. Please God that somebody may find out about him someday.

ADMIRAL FREELAND DAUBIN, USN
Commander of Submarines
in the Atlantic, 1943

The only thing that really frightened me during the war was the U-boat peril.

WINSTON CHURCHILL

THE VAST GRAY shimmer of the North Atlantic did not betray a world at war. The similar gray of the cloud-blanketed sky added to what might have been a gifted Impressionist's seascape; the moon, streaking through clouds, seemed an austerely beautiful sign from a benign God looking down upon a peaceful planet. Not a ripple, in these gently rolling waves, indicated that this was May of 1942; that these waters were a battlefield no less bloody than any other; or that this ocean was as unforgiving as any enemy, swallowing the casualties of either side, equitably.

The man at the periscope knew all this. He was a man who could appreciate the abstract beauty of an ocean quartered by the scale of his viewing lens; but the endless rolling gray seemed to him the color of gunmetal, the mood of the moon knifing through the clouds struck him as foreboding.

And yet he smiled.

He smiled because his periscope—slicing through the waves, a minor disruption in the emptiness of the Atlantic—was revealing a second disruption: the black smudge of a ship silhouetted against the gray sky. Brown-bearded, leather-jacketed, with an oval, intelligent face and the hard dark eyes of a hunter under the black bill of his white cap, the captain of this submarine had sighted his prey. Like the sharks that roamed these same waters, the captain knew he had spied a helpless victim—the horizon revealed no escort—but, like those sharks, he relished this without sadism or self-satisfaction.

The submarine was, by design, a weapon of war whose principal objective was to interrupt shipping—whether naval or merchant. On both sides of this war, the navies exploited the terror that came from the submarine's ability to attack unseen, from below, often at night, not only disturbing but discouraging shipping.

That was this captain's job—every submarine captain's job.

The lack of escort meant the captain and his men could carry out their objective and still survive this night. Attack and survival were, after all, two key rules of the submarine service—perhaps the only rules that truly mattered out here in wet oblivion.

And, so, he smiled.

His was, of necessity, a lonely job. His boat left dock and traveled hundreds, even thousands of miles, to its designated area, working alone, perhaps skulking at a harbor entrance or, as was the case of this patrol, prowling the straits through which ships had to pass. He must be a father to his crew and yet remain aloof and confident, so they would follow him willingly to the death that three of four submariners would meet on, and under, the waters of this war.

Many of his men would not see the sun for weeks, would develop a ghastly pallor and a smell that the occasional sponge bath could not dispel. Their world was little wider than a man's out-stretched hands, a steel tunnel outfitted with pipes and ducts, handwheels and instruments, machinery and weapons. They would endure days and nights of monotony as brutal as combat, standing constant watch, sleeping in their clothes, even sharing bunks, suffering a tedium through which a sub-mariner must remain as alert and exacting at his various jobs as when he set clean-shaven sail weeks before.

That was the other key rule, come to think of it: *no excuses, no mistakes . . . because there were no second chances under the sea.*

The captain allowed himself to feel affection for, but no attachment to, these children. Fresh out of vocational schools, brimming with their new knowledge of mechanics, electricity and diesel en-gines, these boys were younger on average by far than the surface navy, with its reservists and old hands—as young as eighteen, rarely older than twenty-two. At twenty-six, he was the old man of this boat. At the moment, the young crew members were still languishing in boredom, unaware that hell was about to break loose.

Only the man at the periscope, viewing the smudge of a freighter against the sky, knew their boredom was about to shatter like a china plate against a bulkhead. He knew, too, that his craft was as vulnerable as it was deadly, with not only strengths but frailties that required tactical precision on the part of the man in command.

So he waited. And watched. The thrill of the chase his alone—as only he could see the target.

Clutching the periscope handles, grappling with its massive shaft, he shifted it as he peered through the foam-rubber-cushioned eyepiece, the 'scope's motor humming. The icy North Atlantic did not prevent the diesel-tinged air in the sub from being typically stale and hot—sweat beaded his brow, and he drew back, wiping it away, keeping its salty sting from his eyes.

Around him was the nerve center of the steel beast, the Control Room, glutted with valves, tangled cables, white-faced dials, scales and indicators, gray-and-red handwheels, ducts, pipes, switches, meters and a single gyro compass. Here pumps, rudder and hydroplanes were controlled; here, too, were the chart closet and table.

His chief was overseeing the pair of hydroplane operators, intent on their gauges indicating depth and trim. The Control Room mate was at the chief's side, ready to spin air-distributor wheels. At the captain's side was his exec, a lieutenant whose stubble-brushed baby face belied his competence.

In their midst was that umbilical cord to the watery world above, his best friend, his eyes, his periscope. Which he was again gazing through when he said, quietly to the young lieutenant, "Range five hundred meters. Angle on the bow, sixty green. Stand by to mark final bearing—*mark*."

The lieutenant, taking a reading, said, "Zero zero

nine—tracking, sir. Gyros five degrees left."

The captain waited one heartbeat.

Another.

Then, forcefully, he shattered the boredom: "Tube one, fire."

"Tube one, fire!" the lieutenant repeated.

"Tube four, fire," the captain said.

"Tube four, fire!"

Directly above the Control Room, in the iron closet of the conning tower, an officer's fingers flew over the keys of the torpedo computer—a high-speed electronic calculator that transmitted course, speed and range data to the torpedoes in their tubes.

Forward, in the area that served as shared sleeping quarters for crew and torpedoes, all of the men were now awake and, roused by the punch of buttons, so were two torpedoes. The sub shivered as if from the icy waters as, with two bursts of compressed air, it ousted the torpedoes from their beds.

These projectiles—twenty-one feet long, twenty-one inches in diameter—were not so much bombs as smaller subs themselves, unmanned ones, each with an engine, propellers and rudder of its own, carrying no crew or passengers, merely a payload of three hundred pounds of TNT, with a range of seven miles and a speed from twenty-eight to sixty knots, gyroscope wheel awhirl, keeping it on course.

Stopwatch in hand, the captain's exec read off the numbers: "Five, four, three, two, one . . ."

Like rapid strokes from either hand of a marching band's bass drummer, one, two explosions careened through the sea, shaking the ship like a naughty child; but no one minded the rebuke or the reverberation: cheers and applause and whistles resounded down the iron hallway.

The captain, however, said nothing. He just poked the nose of the periscope higher and had a look through its crosshairs to see what he had done to the gray cathedral of the night.

To the cathedral had been added yellow and orange and red stained-glass windows: the horizon was alive with flame, and waves had turned angry, whether by vibration or shift in weather, the captain couldn't say.

He only knew the freighter had embraced both his torpedoes and had cracked in two, like an egg, sinking in halves, spewing a yolk of billowing smoke, thick, nasty, darker than the sky; tongues of fire lashed and licked, still hungry, as if this feast he'd provided was not enough.

The crew's self-congratulatory cheers were still ringing, as the captain drew his face away from the viewfinder and smiled joylessly.

To the men around him, he said, quietly, "We've broken her back."

"Good shooting, sir," the lieutenant said.

The captain twitched another smile.

And then, seemingly from all around them, carried by the sea, came strange shrieks and metallic groans that stopped the cheering and even erased the captain's tiny smile. Not human voices, though chillingly similar, these were nonetheless cries.

"Know what that is?" the captain asked them. "That's the sound of a ship dying."

They would never mistake that for anything else—the breaking up of underwater compartments, the gnashing of steel bulkheads under pressure. . . .

The faces in the Control Room went blank, eyes raised. To the captain, they looked like choirboy faces, cringing at the sound of iron smashing into iron, as if a heavy chain were being dragged across a steel floor and then smacked into a steel wall. The captain's boys shuddered at the squeal of iron buckling, the rumble of engines tearing loose from their housings, the crackle of bulkheads sinking— muffled yet vivid sounds, like tormented souls howling through a haunted house.

From the low, round hatch in the bulkhead, the passageway between the Control Room and the radio shack, the voice of the hydrophone operator rang out: "Captain—contact! Bearing one eight zero!"

The captain spun his periscope, one hundred eighty degrees.

"Fast screws!" the hydrophone operator yelled. "Captain, a destroyer—closing fast."

But the captain already had the bad news within the periscope crosshairs: the freighter had an escort after all, a destroyer whose angry prow was headed straight for them, its searchlights slashing the night.

Slapping its handles shut, lowering the 'scope, the captain issued a stream of orders, all of them echoed by his lieutenant.

"Flood!"

"*Flood!*"

"Forward hard down . . ."

"Forward hard down!"

"Shut torpedo doors . . ."

"Shut torpedo doors!"

"Dive to ninety meters . . ."

"Dive to ninety meters!"

"Helm, right twenty degrees rudder."

"Helm, right twenty degrees rudder!"

Sucking in stale air, the captain maintained calm at the center of the storm of activity around him— his boys, his men, snapping to, wheel spinners, lever pushers, handle turners, planesmen busy at their controls, his chief twisting handwheels with speed and precision.

The captain's eyes raised as his sub nosed down, puncturing the eerie stillness of the sea with its steep dive and electric-motor hum.

Propellers churned the waters above, growing louder, louder, louder still, now accompanied by the relentless *ping-ping-ping* of the destroyer's ASDIC sonar, locking onto them.

They were the prey now, the captain knew; they were the target. Such was war. Time for the reckoning, time for the inevitable.

Time for the depth charges.

"Splashes!" cried the hydrophone operator through the portal.

"Hold on, men," the captain said, and he grinned. "Our friends upstairs are about to take a crap on us."

Nervous smiles flickered on the choirboy faces.

"Hold on to something," the captain advised, and he himself latched on to the greasy shaft of the scope.

A *thump* to the right gave the sub a quaver; the boys looked in that direction. A *thump* to the left gave it another quake, nothing much, just enough to turn the boys' heads the other way. Flakes of paint dropped from the ceiling, clung to shoulders like dandruff. Most of these sailors had not experienced depth charges before, and a few flickered smiles of relief, as if that might be all, as if saying, *That wasn't so bad*.

"Hold on!" the captain said. "They've bracketed us. Next one will be closer."

No one asked, but eyes in baby faces asked, *What can we do, Captain?*

"Nothing we can do but sit tight and take it," he told them. *And feel your guts shrivel up inside yourself and hope to live through the most horrific experience of your life. . . .*

Then someone shot off a goddamn cannon right over their heads, or so it sounded, as a powerful spring drove striker into primer and depth charges exploded with a force that shook sailors like a child shaking candy in a box. Everything loose in the ship went flying, rolling, careening, while cork hull-lining insulation showered them like window-flung confetti hailing heroes on parade.

Then silence.

His boys picked themselves up, touching fingers gently to split scalps, to bloody lips, and the captain gazed around him at dials and gauges whose glass faces had cracked. . . .

Four more blasts bumped the boat—not direct hits, but then direct hits were rare, the captain knew, depth charges, like torpedoes, gaining their deadly effect through the incompressibility of the water in which they exploded.

In this mood of calm reflection, the captain watched as lightbulbs burst like party favors, and chunks of glass and crockery went clattering, the contents of bunks and lockers emptying themselves, and books and phonograph records and navigation books and charts going on wild rides. The captain winced as the ship trembled and creaked and groaned and howled, his boys echoing the boat's pain with their own groans and howls. Then a shaft of seawater lanced through the Control Room, its pressurized stream erupting from a broken hull fitting.

"Stop that leak," the captain said.

And as the boys found a hammer and pounded in a wooden plug, moving quickly, with no visible fear, making him proud, the captain noticed an orange that had rolled in here, presumably from the galley (though food was stored throughout the nooks and crannies of the ship). He plucked the orange from the floor, rubbed oil off it onto his trousers, and took a bite, peel and all—cool, refreshing, sweet, bitter, the taste of it reinvigorated him.

Still alive.

He lent his experienced eye to the gauges, imagining what life must be like right now back in the diesel room—sailors fighting to stop fuel oil and hydraulic fluid spraying from burst pipes, wrenches slipping in their hands, fuel dripping everywhere. His diesel chief would be operating valves, his engineer training a flashlight on work thrown into darkness by broken lightbulbs, cursing men who were working at breakneck speed to move even faster. . . .

"Forward planes neutral," the captain said. "Steady on course."

"Destroyer changing course," his hydrophone operator called out. "Drawing right!"

"Reverse port shaft," the captain said, moving to where his eyes could fix on the gyro compass, "one five zero revolutions starboard. Helm hard port."

He watched the compass as the ship responded to his commands, as if he had spoken to it directly, not through his crew.

"Center the rudder," he said. "All ahead one-third."

Hope colored the hydrophone operator's voice. "Destroyer heading away . . . Screw noise fading."

The captain slapped on a grin, making sure everyone in the Control Room saw it. "They've gone off to do something else in their spare time."

The terrified boys grinned back at him—but with something world-weary in those baby faces, now. They grew old so quickly on a submarine.

No hope could be found in the hydrophone operator's next report: "More splashes!"

"Damn!" The captain felt his forced grin melt to a scowl. "They've left us a few going-away presents. All stop."

"All stop!" his lieutenant said.

Fuel oil leaking had no doubt given their position away. The captain took another bite of orange, a savage one, juice running down into his beard. He didn't bother to wipe it away. The boys around him latched onto anything they could, listening, like he was. Listening, listening . . . listening for the click that would precede the depth charge's detonation . . .

Like a high heel on a polished ballroom floor, it came, a sharp little *klik*, and the captain hugged the periscope shaft, slowdancing, as the ocean exploded, *boom!*, rocking the ship like a hobbyhorse, *klik, boom!*, tossing it like a ragdoll, *klik, boom!*, hurling it like an empty bottle, *klik, boom!*, shaking it like a half-dead mouse in the mouth of a cat, intent on finishing the job.

Glass was shattering everywhere, under the onslaught, faces on gauges shattered, lightbulbs popping, and broken pipes sent water spraying through the Control Room, drenching the planesmen. The skin of the ship groaned and creaked, as the sea itself threaten to crush the sub like an eggshell.

The sound of an explosion aft shook the ship from within—and shook the captain in another way: all the machinery and electrical equipment was back there, the air compressor, the electric motors and their gigantic storage batteries, a torpedo tube and of course the two powerful diesel engines. Those poor bastards back there, God help them. . . .

Screams aft echoed forward, cries of "Fire!," as indeed the flames had engufled the entire diesel compartment, and by the time the electrician's chief, in breathing gear, beat back the flames by poking an extinguisher through the hatchway, every man was dead, a sudden tangle of charred flesh, twisted limbs, teeth clenched in death grimaces.

In the Control Room, latest leak patched, the chief was telling his captain, "One hundred twenty meters."

"Blow one, two and three," the captain said.

"Blow one, two and three!"

"All planes hard rise."

"All planes hard rise!"

Black smoke came pluming down the corridor, streaming into the Control Room. His boys, coughing, climbed into breathing rigs. The captain's nose twitched, and his brain reeled, at the smell, the thought, of burnt human flesh.

"Captain!" the chief yelled. "We're rising fast! One hundred meters . . . Ninety meters . . ."

The junior planesman, who had not taken his hands off his controls to put on breathing gear, coughed and said, "Somebody's dead meat."

"Shut up," the chief said, "or you're dead meat. That's your shipmates, for Christ's sake. Eighty meters!"

"Damage reports," the captain said, again at his periscope.

The clouds had broken—stars glittered, and the moon revealed itself as an ironic smiling crescent. Through his crosshairs he could see the bow of his boat as it bubbled up suddenly out of the water, then the black deck, emerging out of a swirling froth, a sight the captain had seen hundreds of times, and which never failed to thrill him. Then the bow crashed down, the sub wallowing in the waves, and the captain—whirling the 'scope around, searching the sea for company—wondered if they might still have a chance.

"No contacts," he said. "Lookouts to the bridge."

In moments four lookouts, in oilskin rain gear, were clambering up the ladder, bridge hatch opening, water pouring down into the Control Room.

"Why aren't my bells being answered?" the captain demanded.

This was said just as the boy who was his electrician's chief rushed into the Control Room, face sooty, streaked with tears.

"Damage report, goddamnit!" the captain said.

"They're dead, Captain. All dead. From Chief Muller, on down. . . . Port exhaust door failed. Port diesel flooded, crankcase and all. Starboard diesel . . ."

"Batteries?"

"Damaged," the boy sighed. "Three hundred amps forward, two hundred aft. I can jumper out the damaged cells for, maybe, three hundred aft, if we're lucky."

"Well, wouldn't that just be our luck?" The bitterness was as bad as the acrid smell and taste of smoke. "Just enough to keep the lights on, and maybe maneuver a little. What the hell's the use?"

The boy seemed about to cry.

The captain sighed.

"Get us that juice, please," the captain told the boy, gently, hoping to head off the tears. "And set your gang to work clearing out those bodies."

"Yes, sir."

As the young electrician's chief made his way out through the thankfully dissipating smoke, the captain called out, "Radioman!"

"Yes, Captain!"

"Compose a message for Admiral Dönitz."

"Yes, Captain."

"All propulsion systems out, stop." The captain hesitated, then said it: "We are dead in the water, stop."

The boys around him looked at him as if the truth of their situation had not become real for them until their captain finally admitted it.

The same was true for the captain himself.

With that admission, Kapitanlieutnant Gunthar Wassner knew with a sudden strange sureness that the German sub U-571—a VII-C class vessel, 220 feet long, normally capable of 2800 horsepower, harbinger of fourteen deadly torpedoes, currently rolling helplessly in the waves—would likely soon join that freighter at the bottom of the Atlantic.

FOR MAY IN New England, the night was warm, almost balmy, but the ocean breeze drifted in to cool things off, and waft along the strains of "They Can't Take That Away From Me," given a nice brassy big-band lilt by the base jazz band, from within the Portsmouth Officers' Club. The sky— clear and starry with a silver slice of moon—might have been the artificial heavens of some posh nightclub.

Itself fairly posh, considering, the officers' club— into and out of which couples wended, romantically entwined, intoxicated with each other (among other things)—was on Seavey's Island, a large part of which the Navy Yard occupied. The Yard— devoted primarily to the building and repair of US Navy submarines—was not technically in Portsmouth, New Hampshire, at all, rather in Kittery, Maine, across the Piscataqua River. Perhaps the Navy liked the sound of Portsmouth better.

The club—one of many nondescript brick buildings radiating out from around the white colonial house of the commandant—had a well-outfitted bar, a first-class dining room, even a small casino with slots. Lieutenant Andrew J. Tyler had spent many wonderful hours there, thanks to a succession of local girls and Navy nurses, every one of whom had expressed a liking for his faint Texas accent. Betsy had deemed that gentle twang cute, and Margie had spoken of its "subtle music," which had made him laugh.

Tonight, as he pulled into the officers' club parking lot, Andy Tyler wasn't laughing. Nor was he accompanied by a sweet young thing. He was quite alone in the blue '39 Chevy sedan he had brought with him from Galveston. Though suffering the pallor of any seasoned submariner, Tyler was a rawboned, handsome twenty-seven, with a lanky, muscular frame—the accent hadn't been the only thing those girls had been attracted to—and he had a sense of his own good looks and natural charm, and only rarely lapsed into cockiness.

Tonight, however, every ounce of confidence had been drained from him—any sense of self-worth. Gone.

Sitting in the stillness of the parked but idling car, the upbeat brassy big-band sounds floating on the breeze, Tyler—in his dress whites—picked up the letter on the seat next to him. He held it in both hands, as if to read it, but did not look at it, not the short neatly typed message, not even the embossed DEPARTMENT OF THE NAVY letterhead.

He had read it a dozen times already. At least.

And he had spent the afternoon and early evening careening between disappointment, self-pity and indignation.

Muted laughter from the party within the club seemed to mock him, and he folded the letter back up and stuffed it in his inside breast pocket. He looked at himself in the rearview mirror, as if the answer to this injustice—or evidence of his own inadequacies—might be on display.

No help.

A sudden decision made him reach for the gear shift—he wouldn't go in. He wouldn't embarrass himself, wouldn't dignify the man he held responsible with a confrontation. Tyler had a temper, and damn well knew it, and certainly didn't want to spoil things for Lars and his new bride—bad enough their wedding and honeymoon had been crammed into this lousy forty-eight-hour liberty.

Tyler was about to back out when the way was blocked by an officer guiding his tipsy girlfriend behind the car. Their laughter seemed personally insulting to Tyler, somehow. He sighed, watched them in the mirror, caught his reflection again—his tight jaw, muscles working under the skin.

And he turned the engine off, got out, striding past a couple necking under a tree, and headed in.

Lieutenant Pete Emmett was holding court just inside the entryway with some young sailors and their dates. These young sailors had officers' club privileges tonight because of Lars's wedding reception. Tyler knew them all—they were crew members aboard the S-33, where he was executive officer and Emmett was chief engineer.

Probably Tyler's best friend in the Navy, the slim, angularly handsome Emmett, looking spiffy in dress whites, had his arm around a good-looking brunette, a nurse Tyler had never got around to dating, somehow. Emmett vaguely resembled that skinny 4-F crooner, Sinatra, and got a lot of mileage out of it with the cuties.

"There's the man of the hour!" Emmett said, raising a champagne glass.

"Do I look like a groom?" Tyler said, taking off his hat, managing a small smile.

"Looks like you don't even have a bride, tonight," Emmett said. "Slippin', pal o' mine? Where the hell you been, anyway? This is an all-hands function!"

"I got held up."

"Well, grab a lampshade and join the party!" Gesturing to the pretty brunette, Emmett said, "Have you met Joanie, from over at the Naval Hospital?"

"No, seen her around though. Hi."

"Hi," Joanie said, shyly.

"Don't get too friendly with him," Emmett advised her. "He's more dangerous than he looks—this is Andy Tyler, my best friend on land or under the sea. We survived four years at Annapolis together."

Then Emmett produced a twenty-five-cent cigar from nowhere—his magician's moves impressed the girls almost as much as his Frankie Boy mug—and tucked it in Tyler's breast pocket. "Saved you one of the groom's stogies."

"Thanks, Pete."

Tyler gave the little group a cordial smile and was moving on when Emmett's hand gripped his arm.

"You're not gettin' off so easy!" Emmett lifted the champagne glass again. "To the Navy's next sub skipper! Lieutenant Andrew J. Tyler!"

The young gobs joined in, raising glasses, shouting, "Here! Here!" and "Damn straight," and even a few simple hoorays.

Tyler swallowed, nodded his thanks, and moved on. He didn't see the confused expressions he'd left in his wake, but he could feel them, hot on his neck.

Moving through the bar into the dining room, Tyler merely nodded in response to the greetings from his fellow officers and various enlisted men. Herb Griggs, helmsman on the S-33, and a fellow native of the Lone Star state, raised his mug of beer.

"Lieutenant—how about hoistin' a few with us poor enlisted boys?"

Tyler flicked Griggs a smile. "Later."

Moving on, he found his path blocked by fresh-faced Ted "Trigger" Fitzgerald, at seventeen the baby of the S-33.

"Sir, I got my mom here visitin'," the boy said, happy, anxious. "Could I bring her over to meet you, Mr. Tyler? I'd really like for her to—"

"Later," he said.

Only vaguely aware of the confused, even concerned faces he'd again left strewn in his path, Tyler went on into the main dining room, where the portable dance floor had been rolled out and the base band, in their dress blues, were on the bandstand doing a nice swingy job on "Cheek to Cheek." The wood-paneled, curtained dining room was decked out wedding reception style, a drooping banner reading CONGRATULATIONS ENSIGN AND MRS. LARSON.

Officers in dress whites were cutting a rug with their wives or girlfriends, with only a few sailors and their dates joining in. Most of the gobs here seemed to have come stag—Tyler figured attending a party at the officers' club must have made them feel uncomfortable. If his analysis was correct, the sailors seemed to be addressing their discomfort by sitting at tables together getting soused. At any rate, the boys were keeping the Filipino stewards hopping, keeping the cold ones coming.

Lieutenant Commander Mike Dahlgren was dancing with his twelve-year-old daughter, Prudence. Blond, boyishly handsome, with a linebacker's build, Dahlgren was the skipper of the S-33, and at thirty-seven not only the Old Man of the ship (not counting fiftyish Chief Klough, of course), but a true veteran of the submarine service, one of the older captains.

Tyler had always admired Dahlgren's steady bearing; the man fairly exuded experience and authority. It was odd seeing the loving, gentle expression on that farmboy face, as Dahlgren gently guided his daughter around the dance floor. All curls, chiffon and smiles, Prudence beamed at her papa, proud as a princess in his arms.

Funny—Tyler admired Dahlgren even now ... even as he hated the SOB's guts.

Also out on the dance floor was the happy couple, twirling and whirling to that up-tempo "Cheek to Cheek." Fetching in the outfit she'd been married in, a navy dress with lacy white collar and a pleated flounce skirt, Peggy Larson (the former Margaret Jensen) was a blonde knockout who could have given Betty Grable a run for the money. Ensign Keith Larson—Lars, chief petty officer in charge of the torpedo crew—was a dark-haired kid with All-American good looks. Lars, who was another of Tyler's closest friends in the service, looked as happy as Tyler didn't.

If the bride and groom's terpsichorean turn didn't exactly banish the memory of Fred Astaire and Ginger Rogers, they certainly displayed vigor and enthusiasm, as well as (on the bride's part) nice gams. This elicited some wolf whistles and hubba hubbas from a table of well-oiled sailors, which included Charles "Tank" Clemens and Ronald "Rabbit" Parker, of the S-33—machinist mate and torpedoman, respectively.

Their "admiration" caused the bride to blush, and Lars to pilot her away from the clutch of tables where the lubricated enlisted men were seated.

Just as this was taking place, out of the men's room trundled Chief Petty Officer Henry Klough— the S-33's beloved, grizzled chief of the boat, who looked like a cross between James Cagney and Popeye the Sailor. Frowning at the disrespect the bride was receiving, he was already on his way over to chastise the sailors when Dahlgren—who had also witnessed the sloshed sailors' leering behavior—sent the Chief a message . . . an order . . . with the barest flick of his eyes.

Tyler watched as Klough, twitching a non-smile,

hiking up his trousers, strode up behind Tank and Rabbit and the others at the table.

"She's a looker, ain't she?" he asked them, leaning in, flashing a smile that was more a grimace.

"Oh yeah!" Tank said. "Woo woo woo bait!"

" 'Heaven, he'll be in heaven,' " Rabbit sang, getting in on the last verse of "Cheek to Cheek" in his off-key tenor.

Like a light turned off, Klough's smile became a scowl. "Well, she's an officer's wife now. You chowderheads ain't judgin' a beauty show, y'know, or sittin' in the front row at Minsky's. Keep your traps shut, screw your eyeballs back in and anybody puts a paw on the little lady'll pull back a bloody stump courtesy of yours truly."

Normally just the scowl would have been enough. But this time the words didn't work, either. The gobs were still staring, still making the sort of noises construction workers made at a passing filly, when the Filipino steward came over with the latest tray of beers—and, like a traffic cop, Klough held up his hand in a "stop" motion.

"They're officially cut off," Klough said.

And now the sailors turned toward the Chief with apologetic pusses and whiny kid voices, Rabbit saying, "I wasn't lookin', honest," Tank saying, "Not the suds, Chief, anything but the suds!"

Klough grinned now—a real grin—and, with a wink to the steward, turned the suds back on. Swiveling their backs to the dance floor, lesson learned, the gobs gave their full attention to emptying their beers.

Noticing Tyler watching, Klough sauntered over

with all the grace of a bowlegged cowboy.

"Nicely done, Chief," Tyler said.

"Thank you, sir. Quite a night for Lars."

"Lucky man."

"Can't hardly blame the boys for whistling. . . . Everything all right, sir?"

The song was finally over, a slow tune—"I'll Be Seeing You"—starting up. The bride and groom fell into a standing, swaying embrace as the Skipper led his daughter off the floor, winding through couples streaming out to dance slow.

"Talk to you later, Chief," Tyler said. "I need to pay my respects to the Captain."

Klough nodded, smiled, but his eyes were tight. "Yes, sir. Fine man, the Captain."

Tyler said nothing, just moved along the perimeter of the dance floor until he had reached the table where Captain Dahlgren and his redheaded wife, Penelope, sat with their daughter.

"Lieutenant Tyler!" Prudence called, lighting up. She was pretty, like her mother; blonde, like her father. "Come sit with us!"

Tyler had been invited over to the Dahlgrens' on several occasions, and the girl had taken to him, maybe even had a little crush on him. He had thought of the Skipper the way he'd felt about his high-school football coach; and he'd come to regard the Dahlgrens as a sort of second family.

Which was why this cut even deeper.

"Hello, Prudence," Tyler said to the child, but did not sit. "Good evening, Captain."

"Hello, Lieutenant," Dahlgren said. His smile was pleasant enough but his eyes seemed wary.

With a smile and nod, Tyler said stiltedly, "How are you this evening, Mrs. Dahlgren?"

"Why so formal, Andy?" she asked, eyes bright. "And no date tonight? That's not like you."

"I'm afraid I couldn't find anyone on such short notice, ma'am."

"This wedding did take us all by surprise," she admitted, her eyes tightening. She finally seemed to be sensing something was wrong.

"Sir," Tyler said, turning to his captain, "I'm sorry to intrude on your family. But could I speak with you for a moment?"

Dahlgren's smile was gone and the eyes seemed more weary than wary, now. He nodded, excused himself to his wife and daughter, and followed Tyler into the bar just as the band was going on break. A few faces watched this two-man procession with curiosity, as Dahlgren didn't generally follow: he led.

They stood near the bar. Neither man seemed to want to sit at the nearby stools, though they were close enough for Tyler to remove the letter from his inside pocket, unfold it and spread it open on the counter.

Dahlgren did not even glance at the letter.

"Then I'm right?" Tyler said, edgily.

"About?"

"You already know that I didn't get my boat."

"I know. I knew."

Tyler sighed. "Sir, with all due respect, there's only one way I could have been denied this post, at this point in my career."

' Dahlgren nodded. "I withheld my recommenda-
tion."

Tyler had guessed it, had known it, but hearing
the Captain admit as much, so flatly, so unapolo-
getically, hit him like a physical blow. Nausea rose
from his stomach, a terrible bile of disappointment.

Choking on his own words, Tyler asked, "Why?
I thought we were . . ."

"We are friends, Andy. You're not ready."

"Not ready? Sir, I have worked my tail off on
the S-33. You know that I'm qualified in every
area."

"And then some."

"Nobody's scored higher marks on paper, or in
execution!"

"No argument."

"Then how could you throw such a wrench in
the works, Skipper? You know the Navy—it could
be a year, maybe two, before I'm considered for
another command!"

"In wartime, more like six months." Dahlgren's
eyes were hooded. "Andy . . . this isn't about
what's best for your career. It's about what's best
for you right now. And what's best for the Navy."

Tyler was shaking his head. "You should have
told me. Given me some damn warning . . ."

"It wasn't a snap decision. But it's a decision
that I've made, and stand behind—that's part of the
job of a captain, Andy. I don't consider you ready
for an independent command. Accept it. It's done."

"As in, this discussion is over?"

"That's right."

Tyler heaved a sigh. "Very well, Captain. Then

I must respectfully inform you of my intention to put in for a transfer to another boat."

Dahlgren's eyebrows lifted in a tiny shrug. "That decision is yours, Lieutenant."

"Or will you block that, too?"

"No. No, I won't."

Someone was moving quickly through the crowded bar, excusing himself; both men turned and saw an ensign approaching.

"Captain Dahlgren, sir?" the ensign called out, still only halfway across the bar. The ensign was tall and tanned, and stuck out in this group of mostly short, to-a-man pale submariners. Even more striking was the fact that he wore the aiguillete of an admiral's aide.

"Yes?" Dahlgren said, with a puzzled frown.

"Admiral Duke requests your presence, sir, immediately."

The Skipper winced. "The Admiral . . . he's here?"

"Yes, at the Yards, sir."

Dahlgren drew a deep breath, then turned to Tyler, raising a finger in the style of a scolding parent, and Tyler expected one last remark pertaining to what they'd discussed.

But instead the Skipper said only, "I'm counting on you, Andy, to keep the boys out of mischief," and quickly trailed after the Admiral's ensign.

Rug pulled out from under him, Tyler retrieved and tucked away his letter, ordered a rum-and-Coke, and trudged off to meet Trigger's mom and "hoist a few" with the boys.

By midnight the party had wound down—the

band was packing up, the bride and groom had gone off to do what brides and grooms have done since the dawn of marriage, the enlisted men and their wives or sweethearts were off probably similarly occupied, and Tyler was—as his skipper commanded—keeping an eye on the few lingering enlisted men.

Anthony Mazzola, a slickly handsome seaman from Brooklyn, was putting the moves on a pretty, pretty tipsy brunette.

"I know we just met, baby, but things move fast in wartime. When ya feel that special feelin', you gotta seize the moment. I mean, my boat could take a depth charge tomorrow."

She seemed to be just drunk enough to be giving serious consideration to that line of horse hockey. Oddly, so was Rabbit, the little torpedoman mildly crocked himself, seated down the same table, saying to Tank, "You think we could take a depth charge t'morrow, buddy?"

"Oh yeah," Tank said, wiping off his umpteenth beer-foam mustache of the evening, "you betcha, Red Rider—soon as the Heinies invade New Hampshire."

These and the other few remaining boys scattered about the place seemed pretty harmless at this point, so Tyler ambled out to the veranda, where he could sit alone at a table and nurse his latest rum-and-Coke in peace, and smell the ocean, and look at the stars, and feel fucking sorry for himself.

Pretty soon he got around to lighting up that cigar Emmett had given him. It tasted fairly vile but at least didn't explode. Then, suddenly, Chief Klough was sitting next to him.

"Band's loadin' up," the Chief said, and took a sip of beer from a mug. "Keller was too drunk to walk, so I put Lewis in charge of him. Lewis is damn near sober, he'll get the boy back to the barracks."

"Thanks, Chief."

"You wouldn't have another one of those stogies, would ya?"

"Sorry, no. Gift from Emmett. Honor of my new command."

Klough nodded, leaned back in his chair, gazing out at the night.

After a while the Chief said, "Hell, I'm gettin' too old to baby-sit these kids, chase their baby butts around. Shoulda quit ten years ago."

"So why'd you stay in?"

"What else? The pay."

Chief petty officers were selected for their skill at all the jobs aboard a sub, and many—like Klough—were men of long and varied service. Sub pay was fifty percent more than aboard surface ships, plus ten percent for sea duty.

Still, Tyler said, "Pay my ass."

"You're right, sir," Klough chuckled. "Sea's all I know, it's my goddamn life. Besides, it's too early in this war to skip out—I wanna stick around and help you brats put some Kraut tonnage on the bottom, where it belongs."

"Caribbean Station's a hot spot, Chief. We could see some action this time around."

"Shit, sir. It'll be another pleasure cruise, and

you damn well know it. Ain't no way in hell the 33's gonna sink any raiders on that patrol. The most action we'll see is on liberty, hazardous duty gettin' a dose of clap from a busted rubber. . . . Or maybe them Army Air Corps assholes bombin' us on the way down—'Sighted Sub, Sank Same.' "

"You had a few, haven't you, Chief?"

"I have. I have. Sorry, sir."

Tyler shrugged, as if to say, "Don't mention it."

Blew a smoke ring.

Took a sip of his drink.

Said, "Skipper sank me, Chief. Torpedoed me where the sun don't shine."

The Chief said nothing, but the hard dark eyes in the well-creased face were locked onto Tyler.

"Nine months aboard that relic," Tyler said, referring to the S-33. "Doin' the best job I know how, doin' everything once, then twice, making sure I didn't miss anything first time around. You ever see anybody pick up faster on making a submerged approach?"

Klough grinned. "You play a periscope like a harmonica, sir. Beautiful thing."

"Sizing up a target, number of ships in a convoy, direction and speed, position with reference to each other and to us, bearing off our bow, even if they're zigzagging. Knowing just when to fire a torpedo, calculating bearing and range and target speed—"

"Your chance'll come, sir. They're buildin' a new factory, I hear—they ain't makin' nothin' but subs. They'll need you. They'll come to you."

Tyler grunted a non-response to this small comfort. But something in the Chief's voice made Tyler think, *Wait a damn minute here. . . .*

"You knew," Tyler said, eyes wide. "Damnit, Chief, you knew!"

The Chief said nothing. Which confirmed it.

"You coulda told me, Chief. Jesus! You coulda warned me. . . ."

"Not my place, sir."

Klough was gazing at Tyler, sympathetically, but when Tyler searched the older man's eyes, for an opinion on the Captain's decision, he couldn't find one.

Raised voices, a sudden hubbub back inside, in the bar, turned them around, and then—as the commotion escalated—stood them up.

"What the hell?" Tyler said.

"Little late to get lively," Klough said, moving inside, Tyler on his heels.

A half a dozen Marine MPs were rudely rounding up the few remaining patrons, showing them to the door. Tank, Rabbit and the others were too drunk to put up any resistance; and there didn't seem be any fights that were getting broken up or anything. The noise was strictly the MPs yelling: "Club's secured," "Time to hit the racks," "Come on, let's go!"

Tyler went up to the lead MP, a burly Marine with nightstick in hand. "What's the meaning of this, Sergeant?"

"You the senior man?"

"That's right—XO of the S-33. These men have a forty-eight-hour liberty pass."

"Not no more, sir," the Marine said. "Liberty's been cancelled—yours too, sir."

And—after trading bewildered expressions—
Tyler and the Chief headed outside, to help the
drunker boys back to the barracks, wondering exactly what shit had—or was about to—hit the fan.

THOUGH THE PORTSMOUTH Navy Yard, with its over five thousand full-time workers, was primarily dedicated to the repair and building of USN submarines, the islands-spanning facility boasted a stone dry dock that could accommodate a battleship of twenty-three thousand tons, and its trio of mammoth covered buildings could contain vessels up to two thousand tons. Still, subs were the Yard's main order of business, with berths to accommodate over one hundred, and a fitting-out basin large enough to handle ten at a time.

The subbasin was the destination of two troop trucks and an escort jeep, bearing a bedraggled sub crew through a night that had become morning without anyone noticing. The little procession got quickly waved through by a sentry at the checkpoint booth where a Marine rifle squad, barbed wire and sandbags made clear, if anybody hadn't noticed, a war was going on.

Awaiting them at the pier—receiving the attention of two dozen welders and hard-hat workmen toiling for some unknown reason on its conning tower, deck guns and bow—was the salt-caked, white-patched, battered black sewer pipe they called home: the S-33.

This ugly aging whale was a World War One relic, older than everybody on the crew save Chief Klough and maybe the Skipper; its use made as much sense in this new conflict as flying a Fokker or outfitting the infantry in red pants. The S-33 suffered control troubles, engine failures, leaks and fires, but the crew would argue—with conviction and some credibility—that these old overhauled S-boats had been engineered and constructed damn well in their day.

As Chief Klough had been heard to say, when he wasn't swearing at the boat's limitations, "Show her some affection, and this ol' girl'll treat ya right—particularly in the dark. Just don't ask her to do more than she can stomach."

Right now the Chief—one of the first, and most alert, of the crew to pile out of the troop trucks, as they pulled up near the sub—was gawking at his "girl," frowning at the sight of those cutting torches blazing in the darkness, spitting sparks, illuminating the welders' masks with an orange blush.

"What the hell . . ." The Chief had his hands on his hips, head tilted back. "What are those yardbirds doin' to my goddamn boat? *Hey! What are you yardbirds doin' to my goddamn boat?*"

No answer was forthcoming from either the workers, who were making enough noise to have a legitimate excuse, or the sailors, who were staggering around the pier like sleepwalkers.

Lieutenant Andrew Tyler, exiting the other truck,

was equally confused by the conning tower repairs—there had been no damage to it on their recent Caribbean patrol—but knew not to ask such questions. The Navy always had its reasons.

Besides, Captain Dahlgren was standing in the glow of the work above, talking to that admiral's ensign, who was nodding as the Skipper pointed out certain things on a clipboard the ensign held. Something was up. Something big.

A jeep pulled up and an alert Pete Emmett was behind the wheel; riding along were Tank and Rabbit, looking bleary-eyed. Emmett killed the engine and hopped out (and Tank and Rabbit crawled out). Emmett seemed vaguely amused, displaying that same mix of detachment and alacrity Tyler had noted in his friend as far back as their days at Annapolis.

"Hey, Andy," Emmett said casually, crossing to where Tyler stood gazing up at the mysterious repairs in progress. "What do you suppose ComSubPac has up its sleeve for us this time?"

"Some piece of cake or other," Tyler said.

"That sounds about right."

Another jeep roared up and stopped, three Marines escorting the newlywed Ensign Larson.

Lars was hopping mad, and Tyler could hardly blame him, honeymoon night and all—poor bastard.

But Emmett, arms folded, was smiling like a tickled pixie as he watched a Marine try to hand Larson his duffle bag, and Lars just yank it away, glowering.

The Marines in their jeep were pulling away as Lars came over, muttering.

"Jarhead sons of bitches," he was saying, lugging the bag. "Bastards wouldn't even give me five goddamn minutes to consummate my marriage."

"You shoulda asked for two," Emmett said. "All you ever needed before."

"Very funny! Some sympathy I get from you guys!"

"It's between 'shit' and 'syphilis' in the dictionary," Tyler said.

"What is?"

" 'Sympathy.' "

Lars shook his head. "You birds are a riot, a regular four-alarm riot. . . ." Then the ensign noticed the welding going on above, his face flushed with it. "Jesus. What the hell's going on, anyway?"

"Damned if I know," Emmett said.

Dahlgren was striding toward them. "Mr. Tyler! Call the crew to quarters."

"Aye, aye, sir," Tyler said, then turning toward the stumbling sailors—those not half asleep were wholly drunk—yelled, "Quarters! Fall in! Everyone fall in! Get in formation, now!"

Despite their disheveled condition, the sleepwalkers and drunks were transformed, as if by a magician's snap of the fingers, back into sailors. Not surprising to Tyler, not really: the Navy tradition was that only the most intelligent applicants were accepted as submariners, and only men without fear volunteered for such hazardous duty, which only the strong survived. Within seconds they had fallen into tight formation, and Tyler was finishing a quick headcount as the Skipper dropped in at his side.

Tyler swiveled and saluted his skipper. "Captain Dahlgren, all crewmembers are present or accounted for, sir."

"Very well." Dahlgren took a few paces, centering himself before the men. His manner was casual yet firm, professional but not unfriendly. "I'm sorry liberty has been cut short. You deserved a better break than that—we all did. But we have new orders."

Much as he resented Dahlgren right now, Tyler had to admit the man had command presence. His manner, his speech, conveyed how at ease he was with the authority and responsibilities of his job.

"We have two short hours to get stowed for sea," the Skipper said, "and to set the maneuvering watch. Mr. Larson, have your torpedomen load the tubes with their four best torpedoes."

"Aye, aye, sir," Larson said, "our four best torpedoes."

"Mr. Emmett, warm the diesels and line up a battery charge."

"Aye, aye, sir," Emmett said. "Warm diesels and charge battery."

"Mr. Tyler, we have ordnance, dry stores and perishables to get belowdecks."

"Aye, aye, sir. Ordnance, dry stores and perishables will be stowed, sir."

Dahlgren, nodding, cast his eyes upon the face of every one of his men, as if he were scanning the horizon through a periscope for an enemy convoy. Then he said, "Two hours, gentlemen. A minute less, your prerogative; a minute more, unacceptable. Crew dismissed."

And he strode off.

The crew, at ease, began to mutter, to murmur, trading stunned looks of worry, of disbelief.

Tyler was about to light a fire under them when the Chief did it for him, Klough growling, "What the hell are you waitin' for—*please?!* You heard the man! *Stores load!* You got three seconds to get on your boondockers and dungarees and turn to!"

Though most of the sailors were reacting to this like a collective hotfoot, hustling off to their stations, a small clutch of them cornered Tyler, pelting him with questions.

"Mr. Tyler," Mazzola said, "is this the real McCoy or just another damn drill?"

Simultaneously, Trigger whined, "I was supposed to drive my mom home tomorrow!"

And, overlapping Trigger, came Tank's query: "How long we gonna be out on this little pleasure cruise?"

While at the same time Rabbit was sharing his problem: "But Mr. Tyler, all my gear's back in the barracks, all my uniforms, too!"

Holding up his hands in surrender, Tyler said, "Okay, fellas, okay! Let me get the straight dope for you. In the meantime, get to work!"

The little group complied, some of them thanking Tyler, the others just bellyaching some more. Tyler, shaking his head, went after Dahlgren, who seemed to be heading toward a nearby warehouse. This was what he got for being so friendly, so approachable. . . .

"Captain," Tyler said, catching up with Dahlgren, expecting him to stop.

But the Captain kept going.

Tyler fell in alongside him, saying, "Excuse me, sir, but what is this all about? I take it we're not heading back to the Caribbean Station."

"No, we're not." Dahlgren flashed a look to either side of them, and quietly said, "We're going on Special Ops. You're not to be briefed until we're under way."

"Yes, sir. Understood, sir."

And now, surprisingly, Dahlgren halted, Tyler stumbling ahead, and having to back up a step to face his captain, whose professional demeanor had eased, just slightly.

"Andy," Dahlgren said, in the old voice, the friendly voice, "I'm depending on you to put aside our differences for this mission."

"Of course, sir."

"Good. I'm going to expect the very best from you, and the whole crew, on this run. We're clear on that?"

"Yes, sir. Just tell me what you need."

"Well, right now I need Radioman Wentz. Round him up and escort him to the materiels office. . . . And, Andy—when you deliver him, step inside with him." A tiny, enigmatic smile flickered. "My orders specify that your briefing has to wait, but I can at least give you a taste of the seriousness of this assignment."

Then Dahlgren moved on and Tyler was left standing there awkwardly, the conversation having raised more questions than had been answered.

In under three minutes Tyler fetched Bill Wentz from the sailors who, under Chief Klough's direction, had formed a sort of firemen's brigade loading stores onto the boat. Radioman Wentz was twenty-two, blond, with well-chiseled features, a kid from Malden, Massachusetts, near Boston.

"What's this about, Mr. Tyler?" the blue-eyed sailor asked, as the exec of the S-33 walked him over to the massive warehouse inside of which the small materiels office waited.

"I thought maybe *you* knew," Tyler said.

Once inside the tiny office—containing a desk with phone, a few filing cabinets, a handful of chairs, a wall map of the US, another of the Atlantic, and a wall of windows looking out on the supply-stacked warehouse—the seriousness of the matter did, as Dahlgren had indicated it would, present itself.

Standing there with the Skipper, in khakis and garrison cap, was Admiral Duke himself.

Duke was in his late fifties, a trimly fit knife-blade of a man whose hawkish features were softened by kind eyes that were the same steely gray as his hair. Behind the Admiral was a desk where a bookish-looking Naval Reserve officer, a slight mustached man with wire-frame glasses and dark thinning hair, sat, whispering into a telephone, a file folder on the blotter before him. Tyler might have taken him for an aide or a secretary, but the lieutenant had a self-important, intense air that indicated otherwise.

"Mr. Tyler," the Admiral said crisply, extending his hand, which Tyler—swallowing—took and shook. "Good to see you, son. How are you?"

Tyler had been lucky enough to meet the Admiral at the New London Submarine School, the six-month entry gate to the undersea navy.

"Fine, Admiral. Pleased that you remember me."

"I make a point of remembering the men who make top of the class."

Wentz was standing just behind Tyler and hadn't been acknowledged at all—though it had been Wentz's presence, not Tyler's, that had been requested. Curiouser and curiouser . . .

Tyler ventured a question. "What brings you Portsmouth way, sir?"

The Admiral stepped aside and gestured to the professorial Naval Reserve officer, who was still talking on the phone, in a lowered voice, his expression indicating irritation that his important phone call had to be made while another conversation was going on—an interesting attitude, Tyler thought, considering that conversation involved an admiral.

"That's Lieutenant Hirsch," Duke said. "He's going with you on this run. You're not working for Sublant this time around."

Tyler didn't follow this. "He's a VIP passenger, or observer . . . ?"

"No." Duke's eyes may have been kind, but his voice was rock-hard. "He's the boss, son. Mr. Hirsch has operational control. Anything he says goes—anything he wants he gets."

Dahlgren had a glum expression that said he didn't like the sound of that any better than Tyler did.

Hanging up, Hirsch stood—he wasn't very tall, which, considering the accommodations on the S-33, was a blessing—and Tyler held his hand out, saying, "Mr. Hirsch."

Either Hirsch didn't notice the outstretched hand or he was one rude son of a bitch. Instead the reserve lieutenant had his eyes fixed on Wentz, whose presence was finally getting acknowledged.

"Is that him?" Hirsch asked Dahlgren, in a weaselish second tenor.

"That's him," Dahlgren said.

Then Hirsch said, in flawless, unaccented German, "I understand your family comes from Keisblentz, Mr. Wentz. Good Rhine farming folk."

Tyler had no idea what had just been said—but he damn well knew German when he heard it. And it damn near set him on his ass.

But Tyler's reaction was nothing next to Wentz's, whose already pale face turned a whiter shade, his expression suddenly sick. Wentz was trembling, as if he were a German spy who'd been found out.

Wentz a German? Ridiculous. He was from Malden, Mass., for Christ's sake!

"Yes, sir," Wentz said timidly, in English, "I'm from Keisblentz."

Wentz had understood every word! Tyler felt like he'd been hit in the head with a board.

Then Hirsch said, again in a flawless German that was Greek to Tyler (and Dahlgren and Admiral Duke), "Can you speak passable German as well as understand it, Herr Wentz? Can you read and write it? Or are you a simple American farmboy with nothing but the German name?"

And Wentz replied, in an accentless German that surpassed Hirsch's (although of course Tyler didn't know that), "I am a simple American farmboy, yes, Lieutenant. But I speak, read and write German very well. I was studying German literature at Brown when I left to enlist in the fight against Nazism."

Dumbfounded, Tyler didn't know what the hell to think. Neither the Captain nor the Admiral seemed surprised by Wentz's reeling off a paragraph in German. Suddenly Wentz being a Nazi spy seemed slightly less ridiculous . . . slightly.

Hirsch, wearing a patronizing smile as thin as his mustache, looked at the Admiral. "He should do the trick."

Then Lieutenant Hirsch sat back down at the desk—even the Admiral seemed to accept that this low-ranking reserve officer was in charge—and Tyler noticed that the file on the blotter was labeled TOP SECRET.

And Hirsch, with a dismissive nod to the Skipper, was reaching for it.

"That will do for now, Mr. Tyler," Dahlgren said, obeying Hirsch's silent command. "Get back to preparing the boat to get under way."

"Aye, aye, sir."

"You too, Mr. Wentz."

"Yes, sir," Wentz said.

"Pleasure seeing you, sir," Tyler said to the Admiral, and saluted. The Admiral returned the salute, smiled, and turned back to the little man at the desk.

Head spinning, Tyler led Wentz out through the warehouse.

"Mr. Tyler, please," Wentz said, pleadingly. "A moment, please!"

Tyler didn't stop. Though boxes were piled high around them, the glass-and-wood wall of the office they'd just left provided the Admiral, Dahlgren and Hirsch a view of the exiting pair.

But when they were out in the cool darkness of the early morning hours, Tyler paused and said, "Speak your piece and make it quick."

Wentz's eyes were wild, his voice almost shrill. "Please God, don't tell the fellas I'm half-Heinie. They'll hate my fuckin' guts!"

Tyler answered this request with a question: "If it's not top secret, what the hell were you talking about back there?"

Briefly, Wentz explained, concluding with, "I don't know what it's about, though. Who cares if I can speak German?"

Tyler began to walk again and Wentz tagged along. "It's about the mission," Tyler said tersely, "but that's all either one of us knows right now. Which is how it's supposed to be."

"You won't tell the guys, about . . ."

"No. Don't worry, Wentz. Your secret's safe with me—question is, is it safe with that guy Hirsch?"

Wentz's face fell.

Soon they had joined the rest of the crew down the pier. The welding crew was gone, the conning

tower—where most of their work had been done—
covered with a canvas tarp for reasons as yet unex-
plained. The chain of sailors was still hard at work,
snaking supplies up to the after hatch of the S-33—
bunches of bananas, a crate of oranges, boxes of
canned goods (including the ever-popular Spam),
toilet paper, a leg of lamb, a leg of beef, typing
paper, a case of light bulbs, all the necessities and
luxuries needed to make life aboard a sub barely
tolerable.

The Chief seemed to have this firemen's brigade
of foodstuffs and other supplies well under way,
maintaining a good clip. Tyler, brain whirling from
the encounter in the little office, ducked between
the two empty troop trucks for a smoke. He stuffed
a Lucky Strike between his lips but he couldn't
seem to get the damn thing lit, his Zippo sputtering,
as he thumbed the lighter again and again.

Eddie Green, the colored mess steward, came
ambling by, noticing Tyler. "You need a light, Mr.
Tyler?"

"Please." Tyler slipped his Zippo away and the
mess steward stepped forward and lit the Lucky
with a lighter that got flame on the first flick.

"You all right, Mr. Tyler?" Green had the build
of a college fullback but the eyes of a country
preacher.

"Shipshape, Eddie."

"I wanna thank you for that liberty pass."

"Captain's doing."

"Your idea. Hey, and my sweetie thanks you,
too—just too bad those Marines had to come find
us."

"Yeah? Talk to Lars."

Green's laughter rumbled in the night. "Poor son of a buck, on his honeymoon like that. Hope he got the job done."

Exhaling smoke, Tyler said, "I think this hurry-up marriage may indicate the job was done some time ago, Eddie."

Green laughed some more, then seemed to be studying Tyler, who was just starting to feel awkward about it, when the mess steward said, "Listen, Mr. Tyler—just give it time."

"What's that?"

"You're a good man, heart's in the right place. . . . I heard 'bout your disappointment."

Tyler blew out smoke, shook his head. "Hell, everybody know?"

"Naw. One of the advantages of bein' seen but *not* seen, know what I mean, sir? You'd be surprised at the shit I hear."

Tyler had to grin at that. "Don't suppose you know where we're heading?"

"Nope, that one they slid by me—how 'bout you? What do you hear, Mr. Tyler? Got the first faintest foggiest where we're off to?"

"I can narrow it down some."

"Yeah?"

"Not Tokyo."

Green didn't know what to make of that. Then he said, "Hey, I got to get over and lend a hand, Mr. Tyler. I got to make sure those white boys don't break my chicken berries."

Emmett drifted over and said, "Jesus, Andy—

since when am I the last to know? I gotta hear this crap from the Chief?"

"What can I say? Skipper shitcanned me. End of story."

"Give you a reason?"

Tyler shrugged. "Says I'm not ready."

"Not ready? That's horseshit! You want me to talk to him?"

"Yeah, that'll help. He already thinks you're a cocky little prick."

Emmett reared his head back. "*Who's* little?"

Screeching tires caught the attention of both men, and as they looked behind them, a small truck was backing up, coming right at them. As they stepped out of the way, a big redheaded man in a leather flight-type jacket and dungarees hopped out on the passenger side. Even at a bit of a distance, his features were distinctive—sharp eyes, sharper cheekbones and a cleft chin.

Pointing to the S-33, he said, "Either of you tell me where the exec of that hunk of junk's at?"

Though rock-solid-looking, and arriving in a USN vehicle, this guy was not identifiably military.

"That would be me," Tyler said, flipping his Lucky into the night, trailing sparks.

"I need unloading," the guy said, jerking his thumb toward the truck's gate.

Then he reached back and dropped the gate and revealed a full load of large wooden crates; there was something ominous about them—somehow Tyler knew they didn't contain oranges. Pineapples, maybe . . .

"All right," Tyler said. "We'll get to it."

Striding over, the guy twitched a menacing smile. "You'll get to it now."

Emmett—another of Pete's magical gifts was smelling smoldering conflict in the air, and snuffing it before it flared—flashed a friendly smile, stepping between the two men.

"Glad to help, bud," Emmett said. "By the way, who the hell are you?"

"Major Coonan, USMC." He seemed to be going for a weapon under his jacket but came back only with a sheaf of papers, which he thrust at Emmett. "That's the manifest. Get these crates belowdecks, pronto."

"By whose authority?"

"Mine. By way of Lieutenant Hirsch. See, I'm a passenger. You got a problem, talk to him."

Emmett, still smiling, trying to keep a friendly tone, asked, "What is this stuff?"

"My luggage."

Then Major Coonan sauntered off toward the warehouse inside of which was the materiels office.

Tyler and Emmett watched him go.

"Nice guy," Tyler said.

Emmett shrugged. "Couldn't ask to be cooped up in an iron coffin with any better company than that."

"What the hell is going on here? Who's takin' over the Skipper's command, Pete?"

"According to this," Emmett said, waving the manifest, "Office of Naval Intelligence."

"ONI! What's it say is in those crates?"

"Ordnance—how's that for specific?"

Soon the heavy crates from the back of Major

Coonan's truck were being passed along the line, hand to hand. Eddie Green's eggs made it fine, but one of those mysterious crates took a tumble, breaking on the cement, spilling open, solving the mystery.

Thompson submachine guns scattered out on the pier.

"Holy suh-moley!" Trigger said. "It's like Christmas at Al Capone's house!"

That got some laughs, but nervous ones. The glistening steel in the moonlight seemed to wink at the sailors.

"Pick 'em up and put 'em back, girls!" the Chief yelled. "They won't bite!"

But the Chief's eyes held the same wariness as the rest of the sailors.

"Some luggage," Emmett said to Tyler.

"Some passenger," Tyler said.

The work the Captain had ordered done in two hours was done in two hours; the deck had been cleared, cable ends neatly coiled, galley and torpedo hatches shut tight. A bosun's whistle sounded its shrill announcement to prepare for departure. In the predawn darkness, mooring lines were cast off and retrieved, dripping with seawater; diesel smoke belched from the exhaust pipe; water churned and frothed at the sub's stern.

Tyler stood next to Captain Dahlgren on the bridge as the Skipper called out his orders: "Take in all lines! Rudder amidships, all back one-third!"

Soon this relic of the Great War was gliding down the pier, wearing its peculiar canvas-tarp covering over the conning tower, just below them on

the open bridge. Lookouts stood in the crosstrees.
The yawning darkness of the open sea soon swallowed the sub as it cruised easily on the surface,
leaving the lights of the coastline behind.

Down on deck, their "passenger"—the Marine
major in the leather jacket—had commandeered
several sailors on the forward deck. Tyler watched
as the burly major directed the crewmen to slip the
hitches securing the tarp; then Coonan joined in to
help tug the canvas away, dropping the tarp and
every jaw on deck, except Coonan's and Dahlgren's, revealing, at last, some of what the workmen had been up to.

There, welded to the conning tower, washed
ivory in the moonlight, was a shield of sorts, a
grandly painted piece of heraldry including an ea-
gle, crossed swords and, most prominently, a certain all-too-familiar emblem.

A swastika.

Staring like a teenage boy at his first naked
woman, Tyler realized that this shocking crest,
along with other refinements and revisions the
welders and workmen had made to the S-33, had
given the old sub a rather dramatic facelift.

Lieutenant Andrew Tyler was now the executive
officer on what appeared, for all intents and pur-
poses, to be a German U-boat.

THAT THE S-33 was a floating relic, there could be no doubt; on the other hand, every sub in this war reflected a basic design that had remained unchanged since 1905: cylindrical hull pointed at the ends, flanked by ballast tanks; shark-fin-like diving planes at the bow and stern; oil-consuming diesel engines, for travel on the water, battery-fed electric motors for propulsion beneath; and the telescopic device of the periscope, riding up and down in a well through the hull, providing the boat's underwater eyes. Armament remained unchanged as well: deck guns for firing on the surface, torpedo tubes fore and aft when submerged.

Still, Tyler knew nothing could have primed Lieutenant Hirsch and Major Coonan for what must have seemed a descent into hell, as they moved down the ladder from conning tower to Control Room, an impression intensified by the red lighting designed to protect the precious commodity that was night vision. Control Room, crew's mess, wardroom, torpedo rooms, all shifted to red light at sundown, only engineering areas staying white.

Even without the hellish lighting, Hirsch and Coonan would not have been prepared for the plumber's nightmare of the S-33's cramped interior—brass fittings, exposed pipes, a puzzle of tubing and gauges and wire and control wheels. Nor for the ever-present spookhouse-like creaks and squeaks and groans, or the cold dead air with its bouquet of mildew, iodine and dead fish.

And certainly not the casual manner and attire of the crew, boys in blue denim shirts with rolled-up sleeves and dungarees and sometimes even skivvies, milling about with no apparent degree of military order.

As Tyler was giving the two men a quick tour of the boat, numerous crew members spoke to their exec in familiar terms that had Hirsch and Coonan exchanging arched-brow expressions. The news about the swastika on the conning tower had seeped through the boat like a bad leak.

"We're on Special Ops," Tyler would tell them. "That's all I can say, and that's all you need to know."

This was frequently greeted with such responses as, "What a crock of shit!" and "More damn Navy bilge!"

"How can you allow your men to speak to you, as if they were your equals?" Hirsch asked as Tyler led them aft.

"We live together in each other's laps for months on end, Mr. Hirsch. Certain formalities, in lull times, slip away. By normal military standards, I suppose we're an undisciplined bunch."

"No 'suppose' about it," Coonan said. "I've

never seen such a lot of sloppy sailors."

Tyler stopped and looked back at his two charges. "You've never seen any more disciplined sailors, Mr. Coonan. Every man on this boat has to know not only his own job, but every other man's, from grease monkey to navigator. To stay alive, every one of 'em has to perform his tasks under any circumstance, in the same unvarying fraction of a second—or we're all dead."

The tour did not take long. From the foot of the conning-tower ladder, all of the S-33 was visible through a series of open doors, from forward torpedo compartment to aft engine room. The most elaborate explanation was reserved for the controls of the head.

"Nineteen steps, gentlemen," Tyler said. "Follow them in the order as posted, or risk riding a geyser."

Hirsch's eyes were wide as he leaned into the little toilet and read: "Discharge valve 'A' . . . Gate Value 'C' . . . Lever 'A' . . . air-supply line . . . This is ridiculous!"

"Anybody can learn to dive a sub, Mr. Hirsch," Tyler said. "But when you can master this important tactical operation, you may consider yourself a submariner."

Finally Tyler filled them in on the Control Room, where Captain Dahlgren was on the periscope, oblivious to his guests, Chief Klough keeping a general eye on things. Tyler pointed out, on the port side, behind the ladder, the depth gauges and apparatuses that worked the diving planes; forward of these was the panel of red and green indicator lights known as the Christmas Tree, covering every vent and valve in the ship. The forward bulkhead was consumed with sounding gear, speed indicators and motor and engine controls. The starboard side was home to electrical meters, fuse boards, compressed-air manifolds and pump controls. Just behind the engine-control boards were the gyro compass and electrical steering lever.

"Got that?" Tyler asked the two men.

Hirsch and Coonan exchanged quick, blank glances, and nodded.

"Rig for dive," the Skipper said.

Chief Klough spoke into the intercom hand mike: "Rig for dive!"

"Keep out of the way," Tyler advised them, picking up a clipboard from the small desk along the aft bulkhead, "and grab each other if you like—but don't touch anything else."

The two passengers looked as if they wished they could disappear—which was probably the first thing Tyler had agreed with them on.

Through the open passageways the transformation could be seen: Eddie Green, the mess steward, carrying two cups of coffee, slung them onto his right forefinger and reached up with his freed-up left hand to twist a copper wheel, closing a vent—not spilling a drop of the java; a technician in the bow torpedo room was slipping headphones on; the "black gang" was pouring into the motor room, aft; all over the boat men took their positions at valves and switches.

Materializing onto the deck, officers and sailors assumed their posts: Mazzola and Griggs suddenly seated at the diving planes; Chief Klough was minding the Christmas Tree; Pete Emmett was at the speed indicators and motor and engine controls, and nearby Trigger had slipped on headphones at the sounding gear. Ensign Larson's watchful eyes were on the gyro compass, his hands on the steering lever.

"Main induction indicates shut," the Chief said.

"Aye," Emmett said. "We have a green board, Skipper."

This meant there were no red lights lighted on the panel that was the Christmas Tree.

"Rigged for diving," the Chief said.

Larson, having shifted to the chart table, was plotting their position. "Passing the hundred fathom curve, sir."

"Very well," Dahlgren said, eyes still buried in the periscope's padded viewer. "All ahead two-thirds."

"All ahead two-thirds!" Tyler said.

"Mr. Emmett," Dahlgren said, "take us down."

"Aye, aye, sir," Emmett said.

"Make your depth one five zero feet. Ten degrees down bubble."

"One five zero feet, aye. Ten degrees down bubble, aye, sir."

"All ahead two-thirds," Trigger said.

"Chief of the Watch," Emmett said, "diving the ship. Pass the word over the 1MC. Open main ballast tank vents."

Chief Klough had already grabbed the intercom hand mike. "Aye, sir, passing the word. *Dive, dive, dive!*"

The Chief triggered the diving alarm, sending

two strident klaxon bleats, *AAW-OUGAH!*, *AAW-OUGAH!*, echoing through the ship. Then Klough turned several vent valves as Emmett played valet, helping the Skipper into raingear, rainhat and all. This seemed to puzzle and trouble Hirsch.

"Sir," Klough said, "main ballast tank vents indicate open."

"Aye," Emmett said, already back at his indicators and controls. "Both planes fifteen degrees dive."

"Planes fifteen degrees dive, aye," Mazzola said, as he and Griggs turned their wheels.

At the periscope, the rainhatted Dahlgren, looking like he walked off a Morton's Salt ad, said, "Decks awash."

Hirsch was standing near the chart table, where Larson brushed away a cockroach getting in the way of his position reading.

"Mr. Hirsch," the Skipper said.

"Yes, Captain?"

"The hurry-up nature of this mission means the relief crew didn't have the time to do the necessary maintenance work, after our patrol. We're going to take her down a ways, to see what kind of shape she's in."

"This impacts our mission how?"

Dahlgren's smile was so faint, only the crew members recognized it. "If we don't sink, we can carry it out."

Gathering what the Skipper was up to, Tyler sent for Tank. The oversized machinist mate would come in handy if they started springing some Control Room leaks.

Tyler had great respect for these monkey-wrench mechanics who could make makeshift repairs on the fly that were nothing short of miraculous—fashion watertight patches out of paint-soaked canvas, turn rags and tar into cable insulation, make new insides for gauges out of bits of tin and clock parts.

Soon Tank was gently tapping pipes with a small hammer, testing their soundness, like a doctor checking a patient's knee for a reflex action. Tyler smiled to himself, noting the tough Marine, Coonan, staring uneasily up at the overhead hatch, which was bleeding water, apparently wondering why no one else seemed troubled by it.

Emmett noticed, too, and said, "First time on a sub, Major?"

Coonan nodded.

"Sixty feet," the Chief said, reading a depth gauge.

The reason for the Skipper's raingear became apparent as water began showering down from what Tyler knew to be an aged periscope seal.

"Lowering 'scope," Dahlgren said, and the periscope hissed down into its well.

"Captain!" Trigger said, intently listening to a report coming in over his headset. "Engine room experiencing minor flooding from the shaft seals and brine pump. Bilge at eighteen inches and rising."

Unruffled by this news, Dahlgren merely nodded.

Frowning, clearly both frightened and irritated, Hirsch asked, "Why are you doing this, Captain?

You could be endangering the mission."

"If this boat isn't seaworthy, there is no mission."

Hirsch didn't challenge that. Next to him, Coonan's mask of invincibility had slipped badly.

"Captain," the Marine asked, "how deep can this vessel go?"

"Straight to the bottom, Mr. Coonan, unless we stop her. We try not to go beyond a hundred and fifty feet. Any deeper and the leaks might overwhelm our pumps."

As if to underscore the Captain's statement, the hull groaned, protesting this treatment. Sprays of water began to appear here and there, like a weak sprinkler system trying to put out a nonexistent fire, as Larson shielded his chart from the wetness.

The two passengers were obviously unnerved, Hirsch's eyes flitting like those of a man suddenly realizing he had claustrophobia, sweat trailing down Coonan's forehead like he was springing leaks himself.

"One hundred feet," the Chief said.

Tank was tapping a pipe with his hammer, one, two, three, four taps . . . then the fifth was more a *squish*, as the hammer pierced a rusty pipe wall, sticking there like a steel fang, saltwater bubbling out around it.

"Whoops," Tank said, biting his lip. "I better patch this mamma, Skipper."

"Yeah," Dahlgren agreed, "and lash it with marlin. The Yard can fix it when we return to port."

Suddenly the room was illuminated, bathed in white.

"What the hell is that?" Hirsch said.

Tyler thought the guy might jump into the Marine's arms.

"Dawn," Tyler said. "That's when the red lights go off and white ones come on. Cup of coffee, gentlemen?"

And the two passengers nodded, eagerly following Tyler out of the Control Room, not seeing the grins they left in their wake.

By midmorning—the S-33 cruising along the surface now—the tiny area that was the officers' wardroom played host to Tyler, the Skipper, Hirsch, Coonan, Emmett and Larson. On two sides of the twelve-by-eight room were bookcases, and a battered phonograph rested near the chronometer locker. The six men stood around the green-baize-covered table at which meals were served and cards and chess played; at the moment, a chart of the Atlantic was spread out over it like a paper tablecloth.

But neither nourishment nor recreation was at hand.

"Gentlemen," Hirsch was saying, eyes hard behind the wireframes, "I cannot overemphasize the secrecy of what I am about to share with you. This is information known only to a select handful, including the President himself."

Lieutenant Hirsch and Major Coonan were businesslike, now, and—if not exactly friendly—had dropped their air of condescension, having already learned a few small lessons aboard the S-33.

Tapping the chart, Hirsch said, "Yesterday at

0200 hours, right here, a U-boat sank a freighter transporting war refugees. A British destroyer sighted the sub's periscope and dropped depth charges. The U-boat was reported destroyed."

"On what evidence?" Larson asked.

Coonan said, "Breaking-up noises and loss of sonar contact."

Emmett laughed humorlessly. "That's piss-poor confirmation."

"You're right on target, Lieutenant," Hirsch said. "Several hours later, Allied direction-finding stations triangulated a coded enemy radio signal"— he tapped the chart again—"here, near the Chop Line."

"Not sunk," Larson said. "Disabled."

"That's our supposition, yes," Hirsch said. "The U-boat appears to be drifting eastward on a four-knot current."

Tyler asked, "Why is a disabled U-boat of importance to Naval Intelligence?"

"Because *this* is on board," Coonan said, and he passed around a grainy black-and-white photo of an object that appeared not only harmless, but mundane.

"A typewriter?" Larson asked, with a smirk, passing the photo around.

"That," Hirsch said, "is an Enigma encryption machine. With that 'typewriter,' the German Navy communicates with its submarines in secret. And our inability to decipher their coded messages is costing us this war."

Without looking at it, Dahlgren—already briefed on the mission—passed the photo on to Tyler. The code machine did look like a typewriter, in a simple wooden case. The damn thing looked like a college kid's portable Royal! This hunk of junk could determine the outcome of the war?

Hirsch gestured to a harbor on the French coast. "French Resistance reported a resupply sub sailing from the Lorient U-boat pens yesterday afternoon, loaded with engine parts, with a brace of mechanics for passengers."

Tyler said, "A repair ship?"

"A repair ship—going to rendezvous with the disabled U-boat. But not if we get there, first."

Emmett was grinning. "I see what you guys are up to, sticking a swastika on our old All-American girl. Why, it's the goddamn Trojan horse!"

Coonan nodded, grinned a little himself. "We don't claim it's a new idea—just a good one. The S-33 will rendezvous with the U-boat, posing as the German resupply sub. I will lead a boarding party, in Kriegsmarine uniforms, onto the enemy submarine."

Dahlgren spoke for the first time, his expression somber as his eyes traveled over the faces of his men. "Taking it by force, securing the Enigma."

A sick feeling crawled into Tyler's stomach.

"Any German survivors will be transferred to the S-33 and the U-boat will be scuttled," Coonan said.

Emmett's grin had vanished, and Larson was frowning.

Hirsch said, "The German resupply sub will arrive at the rendezvous point and assume the U-boat succumbed to its wounds, and sank." Slowly the Naval Reserve lieutenant scanned the faces of the

S-33 officers. "Gentlemen, the Germans must never suspect we have the Enigma. That is key. Vital. Imperative."

Silence shrouded the little wardroom.

Then Emmett said, "So it's a race?"

"Yes, in effect."

Tyler asked the question to which he dreaded hearing the answer: "Who's the boarding party?"

Looking right at Tyler, Coonan said, "With the exception of Captain Dahlgren, who will remain aboard the S-33, you are. You, Mr. Tyler, as the XO, Mr. Emmett, Mr. Larson, plus Mr. Hirsch and, obviously, myself—and nine of your ship's company, including our German speaker, Radioman Wentz."

Tyler looked toward his friends, Emmett and Larson, who wore pale, sick expressions. When he turned to Dahlgren, he saw, at first, a blank acceptance; then—as though the Skipper could read Tyler's thoughts—Dahlgren nodded, as if to say, *Speak your mind.*

After taking a deep breath and letting it out, slow, Tyler said, "Mr. Hirsch, with all due respect—and please don't misunderstand me—I would ride this boat through the gates of hell and sink a torpedo in the devil's hindquarters, if it would help us win this war. But the boys of the S-33 are submariners . . . sailors . . . *not* combat Marines."

Coonan's voice was surprisingly gentle. "You won't be up against combat Marines, Mr. Tyler. The boys on that U-boat are sailors, too."

"You make this sound so damn easy, Major. You

expect me to stand by and watch my boys get thrown in a meatgrinder and chewed to hell?"

Coonan's gaze was steady, unblinking. "Your men will be ready, Lieutenant. That's part of why I'm here—to train them."

"Major," Emmett said, sitting forward, "we're only four days from the Chop Line."

"Plenty of time."

Emmett laughed, hollowly, and Larson was shaking his head. Tyler just sat there, feeling numb.

Dahlgren straightened and said, "Mr. Hirsch, why don't you tell these men what you told me."

Hirsch bristled. "Captain, don't ask me to share information that is not needed for carrying out this mission."

Dahlgren locked eyes with Hirsch, and said, "Level with these men. You won't be sorry."

Unsure, Hirsch turned to Coonan, who shrugged.

Then Hirsch sighed heavily, and said, "Last month Hitler's U-boats sank a hundred and thirty freighters up and down the East Coast—right off our own coast, gentlemen. We're losing thirty ships a week."

Tyler felt a sickness in his stomach again; but it was different this time.

"If this continues," Hirsch was saying, "England will fall, and we will have to accept a negotiated peace with Nazi Germany. 'Deutschland Über Alles' will replace 'The Star Spangled Banner' at ballgames, and school kids will start their day saluting the Führer, not the flag."

"No offense, Mr. Hirsch," Emmett said, "but aren't you being just a wee bit melodramatic?"

"That's not my assessment, Mr. Emmett. It's the view of the Secretary of War and the President himself. We have a chance to prevent that 'melodramatic' scenario from happening. *You* have that chance."

Tyler glanced at Emmett and Larson, saw the resolve there, exchanged nods with them, and smiled half a smile, saying to Hirsch, "Lieutenant, you came to the right boat. We're used to taking chances."

IN THE FORWARD section of the German submarine, U-571, across from his own small compartment, Kapitanlieutnant Gunthar Wassner stood leaning against the bulkhead beside the nook that was the sub's radio room. In his gray work-worn leather jacket slung over a yellow turtleneck, cap pushed back, dark-blond beard immaculately trimmed, Wassner was the picture of a controlled, composed U-boat captain; but his gut was tight, his insides coiled with impatience, his mind flickering with the fire of his concern for his boat, and his men.

The jumpsuited radioman, a bearded boy of nineteen, sat in his open cubbyhole with only one of the listening gear's earpieces covering an ear, so that with his uncovered one he could hear both incoming Morse signals and orders from within the boat. The clunky-looking Enigma decoding unit, in its pine case, sat before the radioman like a typewriter challenging a novelist with writer's block.

Three messages had come in today—another U-boat ordered to shift its position westward eighty miles; news of a convoy, too many days' sailing from the U-571 to be of interest (even if the boat had been up and running); and maneuvering instructions for a boat operating in the area of Gibraltar. Back at the commander in chief's headquarters, little flags on a big map, like pieces on a game board, were no doubt being moved to reflect radio reports from subs on patrol.

In the meantime, the U-571 drifted in the current, crippled, helpless, a floating target.

This was an unacceptable state to the U-boat captain, and he was doing everything he could to rectify it—however, there was only so much he could do, and his frustration was bubbling into a barely controlled rage.

Which was another unacceptable state to Wassner: he must set the example for his young crew; any show of anxiety on his part would spread like disease. Earlier today he had allowed himself to lose his temper, and nearly struck one of these boys, back in the diesel room.

The strapping young planesman, face and hands black with grease, had tightened one last bolt inside the starboard diesel, his repairs apparently complete.

"Okay, Chief," the boy had said, with pride, "she is ready for a test."

Wassner and his electrician's chief, at the nearby control panel, had exchanged tiny hopeful smiles; a small audience of sailors looked on anxiously. Then the chief's fingers flew over buttons, and his hands twisted open a valve . . .

. . . and the pistons, encouraged by compressed air, began to rise and fall!

At first, they chugged in a slow, building rhythm; then they began to pick up speed, like a train leaving the station. The electrician's chief shot the captain a tiny smile and Wassner, nodding, smiled back. The grease-smudged boy was grinning, basking in his accomplishment.

Then, expressing its own contrary opinion, the engine began to cough, spewing smoke, shaking as though nervous, running sluggishly now, choppily, losing rhythm, grating, rasping, slowing—and, finally, with a sigh of black smoke—stopping.

Wading through the fumes, Wassner cornered the young planesman, leaning in, nose almost touching the boy's.

Shouting right in his face, Wassner swore and said, "I thought you said you were a mechanic!"

"C-captain," the boy said, blinking, backing up against piping, "I am a mechanic. I apprenticed in my uncle's garage—fixing motorcycles!"

Wassner had brought his hand back, but he didn't strike the lad. Instead, the captain had patted him on the shoulder, nodding at him. The boy had tried. He had tried.

The staccato sound of Morse code broke into Wassner's thoughts, and brought him back to the radio room and the bearded boy wearing the off-kilter headphones, a lad eagerly copying down this latest message, a series of random letters, onto the special form.

When the transmission ended, and the final letters were scribbled down, the radioman flipped

open the nearby codebook, turning to today's date—
15 May 1942—and his finger found the current
four-letter code: FMOX.

Three disks side by side sat in the machinery of
the Engima decoder, edges out, like little phonograph records in a jukebox, edges out and bearing
the alphabet; the radioman thumbed these silver
wheels to bring the letters FMOX into juxtaposi-
tion. The boy began typing the Morse message,
seemingly random letters, on the Engima's keys.

A panel in the machine lighted up and the de-
coded message crawled across. Wassner leaned in
to see, copying the unscrambled text onto a page
of an open notebook: "Wassner—Report your grid
position. Help is approaching. We must have you
fighting again. BDU."

Relieved, Wassner scribbled a reply, directed to
Admiral Dönitz, and handed it to the bearded boy
to encode.

Just as the boy was beginning the painstaking
process of enciphering Wassner's words into apparent gibberish, a bell began to sound and ominous red lights flashed.

"Alarm!"

The dreaded word came echoing down the boat,
his exec's voice, emanating from the Control
Room, where within seconds Wassner had gotten
himself, vaulting up the ladder to the bridge.

He emerged to join Lieutenant Kohl (his exec),
and three raingear-attired lookouts, in the cool sea-
kissed sunny afternoon, the kind of pleasant day
God surely did not design with war in mind. One

of the lookouts was poised at the deck gun, a belt-fed MG-34.

That formidable weapon was trained upon a wooden boat.

Wassner held out his hand and his exec filled it with a pair of Zeiss binoculars. The captain had a closer look at the approaching vessel: a lifeboat, a rather small, pathetic craft charred by fire, with—he counted heads—twelve passengers, bedraggled sailors with soot-smeared faces, in tattered uniforms, the motley survivors of a torpedoed freighter, no doubt. Several were wounded, wrapped in makeshift bandages; all of them looked shell-shocked.

And relieved, pleased to see salvation in the form of the submarine, happily, almost giddily, rowing toward the U-571.

"British," he said.

With a world-weary sigh, Wassner lowered the binoculars. The breeze carried the sound of their rowing across the water, and elated voices.

"Ahoy, friends!" came the spokesman's too cordial, desperation-edged call. His British accent lent a painfully cheery tone to his words. "*Guten Tag! We are in need of aid! We have no food or water!*"

The boys on the bridge of the U-571 turned to Wassner; they did not understand English, but knew he did. Yet Wassner did not reply, instead lifting the binoculars again, searching the horizon, to see if there were other survivors afloat. No. Just this pitiful craft with its pitiful passengers.

"We have many wounded!" the spokesman cried. He was a plump clean-shaven man in his forties with ruddy cheeks; the ship's cook, maybe. "We are merchant seamen, noncombatants! Take us prisoner, please, Herr Kapitan! We'll be no trouble!"

"What did they say, Captain?" Kohl asked.

"They would come aboard and keep us company."

"Do we have room for prisoners, Captain?"

"Of course not." To the lookout on the deck gun, Wassner said, "Shoot them."

The lookout on the machine gun gasped, turning to his captain, surprised and dismayed by this casual, heartless order.

The wooden lifeboat had drifted closer now, the passengers in it more real, more distinct, the signs of their suffering unmistakable, the hope and anguish in the pale faces, bandages over the oil-blinded eyes of several, torn uniforms black with dried blood and fire-scorch.

"Give us a hand, for the love of God!" the spokesman cried. "It's the law of the sea!"

This was not good. Wassner knew his young crew had done its previous killing long-distance; they had not had to face the flesh-and-blood reality of their victims. Time for a hard but necessary lesson in war.

Grabbing the young lookout by the arm, Wassner glared into gentle light-blue eyes in a face unbearded because puberty had barely passed.

"We do not pick up survivors," the captain told the boy, and everyone else on the bridge. "That is the Führer's order, and it's a good one."

The boy swallowed. "Must we . . . kill them, sir?"

"If I had engines," Wassner said, still gripping the lad's arm, "I would leave them to the ocean. But I do not have engines—and if those men are rescued, they will eagerly report our position. The choice is simple—they die, or we die."

Wassner let go of the boy.

The lookout held his captain's gaze, swallowed, then turned to his machine gun. His expression wooden, the blue eyes glazed, the boy cocked the big weapon, swung it toward the lifeboat.

The spokesman's reply to this action might have been amusing, with its politely British, tea-time delivery: "Terribly sorry! We'll just be on our way then. *Danke schön*, my friends. We'll say we never met! By your leave, then . . ."

But there was nothing funny about the way the rowers were so frantically, desperately attempting to take their leave, the joy and relief in faces replaced by terror and despair, their pitiful situation turned tragic.

The blue-eyed boy did not blink, as robotlike, he held steady though his weapon shook with deadly force, hurling bullet after bullet, an endless burst of automatic gunfire, a shocking thunder in the quiet afternoon that almost drowned out the screams and wails and shrieks and the splash of water and the brittle crunching of bullets chewing up wood.

Almost.

The lookout swallowed, numbly; he had zipped through an entire belt, empty shell casings raining onto the deck. The boy stared out at what he'd done, at the wreckage floating on the sea.

Bits and pieces of the wooden craft bobbed and drifted, like a child's toy boats in a bathtub. The biggest piece of the shattered lifeboat was sinking, slipping under the surface, as were the bloody bullet-shredded corpses, and the occasional severed limb. Soon only one of the merchant seamen remained, buoyed by his life jacket, a dead man waiting to be rescued.

The only sounds were the loll of waves and the tinkle of shell casings, rolling on the deck. Wassner's young exec, Kohl, turned away and leaned over the side and lost his breakfast and lunch. The lookout, the boy at the MG-34, was still staring out at that final floater, spinning slowly in his life jacket.

Wassner put a hand on the boy's shoulder, squeezed.

"I'm proud of you son," Wassner told him.

Then Wassner got quickly below, so that if the boy wept, it would not be in front of his captain. To subject the young lookout to that would be too cruel.

ON THE AFTERNOON of the day of the mission, Lieutenant Andrew Tyler—bearing a clipboard with the latest chart positions as calculated by Pete Emmett and his parallel rulers—moved down the brightly lighted passageway, toward Captain Dahlgren's cubbyhole "stateroom." Tyler felt as if he were locked in a surreal dream, these last few days a bizarre blur.

Sanity and order were maintained on a submarine by an almost religious obedience to routine—that was the way things got done safely, minimizing both effort and confusion. On the S-33, like any USN sub, activities were carried out exactly the same way, on the exact same schedule, time after time, day after day. Voltage and temperature readings, watches relieved, logs written, positions recorded, meals prepared, with no orders given for any of that, tasks carried out almost unconsciously. Seldom was anything forgotten, or done wrong.

This seemingly mind-numbing routine was both comforting and necessary, allowing officers and senior petty officers to focus on the larger tasks at hand, and for everyone to be ready to snap to when the klaxon signaled an alarm or a dive.

These last few days, however, had been anything but routine. A school of weapons handling had been conducted by Major Coonan, a college of combat held in the worst possible classroom: the cramped conditions of their old S-boat. U-boat blueprints had been spread out on the steel table of the crew's mess, in the afterbattery compartment, as the major worked separately with his two strike teams (one led by Coonan, the other by Hirsch, who was absent from these sessions, holding down a post in the radar room).

"The U-571 carries forty-four men," Coonan told them. "Our two teams will approach the U-boat on inflated rafts, forward and aft of the conning tower. Our objective is to eliminate the lookouts and get belowdecks before the rest of the German crew knows what's up. Remember, once you're inside, you'll be in close quarters and surrounded by metal. Ricochet factor is critical—do not fire your weapon unless you absolutely have to."

Seeing sailors like Mazzola, Tank and the painfully young Trigger gathered around like schoolboys, listening to this hardened Marine veteran explaining attack tactics, was both absurd and frightening to Tyler. Trigger looked like a kid listening to a Junior G-man show on the radio. Mazzola's prior knowledge of tactical warfare and hand-to-hand combat was limited to maneuvering some skirt into the sack. And if Tank's forehead had clenched any tighter, in an attempt to think, his skin might have fallen off.

Then there were the Nazi fashion shows, guys like Griggs and Rabbit and Wentz tearing open butcher-paper-wrapped packages like kids at Christmas, finding German naval uniforms and shiny black boots, inside. The guys joked like kids in a high school play, as they tried on the uniforms, Griggs babbling on about how back in Texas, they'd shoot him with a hunting rifle, if they saw him in these damn Natsy threads; but Chief Klough watched this display, quietly aghast, seeing nothing funny about it. At all.

Mazzola, looking pretty spiffy in his uniform, shot a sideways glance at Wentz, who seemed uneasy in his, and said, "Always knew you were at least half Kraut."

This was meant as a joke, apparently, but it was a mean one, and Wentz snapped back, "Tell it to your pal Mussolini, greaseball!"

A fight might have broken out, if the Chief hadn't stepped between and told them both to shut the fuck up.

"Next man who spouts off," Klough said, a hand on either man's chest, "is volunteerin' to white-glove the shitter—and I ain't shittin'."

That shut that down; but the near spat was an example of the surreal place the S-33 had become. The crew members almost never fought, every argument a kidding one; you only survived in the restricted world of these iron pipes by having a mutual tolerance that made a monastery look like a free-for-all. These guys loved each other—when shore leave came, and a few hours of privacy was possible, they were still thick as thieves, seldom out of each other's company.

Tyler had heard a war correspondent comment to Dahlgren that the men on subs behaved like family. The Skipper had laughed, harshly.

"If we acted like families act," Dahlgren had told the reporter, "we'd be at each other's throats in days."

The change of routine, the prospect of close-quarters combat, had put more strain on the ship than a two-hundred foot dive. Heading down the passageway, Tyler slowed to acknowledge Lars, who was writing a letter in his bunk; but the ensign turned his back, cupping a photograph protectively in his free hand. This was, no doubt, a snapshot of his new bride, and Lars wanted to be alone with her, and his emotions.

Tyler could hardly blame the guy; but heading into this mission, these men, who had grown so close, needed to be closer still. The rule he'd heard since submarine school, which had been proven again and again on the S-33, was: "If I botch my play, you'll botch yours. You botch yours, and it's deep six for everybody." Out on those rafts, attempting to board an enemy submarine—even more so than on the S-33—they would depend on each other for their lives.

The boat was riding kind of rocky at the moment, and Tyler almost lost his footing. Right now Trigger, Rabbit and Mazzola would be up on the bridge, above the conning tower, no doubt getting good and plastered by waves and wind, raingear or no. Tyler wondered just what exactly the S-33 was cruising into. . . .

At Dahlgren's stateroom, Tyler knocked on the bulkhead.

From within came the Skipper's voice: "Come."

Tyler drew back the curtain on the compact cubbyhole that served as the Skipper's combination office and living quarters. Dahlgren was seated at the fold-down desk, above which was the phone receiver of the intercom; he was writing in the ship's log. Within this tiny closet were crammed a berth, lockers, hot and cold running water and a compass—the best billet on the boat, and quite wretched.

Looking up from his log, Dahlgren said, "Yes, Lieutenant?"

Standing in the passageway (only room for one in the cubbyhole), Tyler handed the clipboard forward. "Our position, Captain."

Without taking it, Dahlgren took a look at the extended clipboard, examining Emmett's handiwork. "Looks like we're still bucking that headwind."

"Yes, sir. I estimate us three hours behind schedule."

Dahlgren's eyes traveled from the clipboard back to his log and he began writing again.

Tyler said, "I told Mr. Emmett to run at flank speed and hold off on a trim dive until we've made up the lost time."

"Fine, Lieutenant," Dahlgren said, not looking up from his writing. "Is there anything else?"

"No, sir."

Tyler had just started to go when Dahlgren's voice reached out for him—the old voice, the voice of a friend.

"Andy!"

"Yes?"

Tyler turned back to his skipper, whose attention was no longer on the logbook, his expression almost warm.

"Andy, God knows you're a first-rate XO. I certainly never had anybody to rival you—and I served with some fine XOs in my time."

"Th-thank you, sir."

"A good XO, a really first-rate one, is hard to come by in this man's navy. You ought to keep that in mind."

Tyler said nothing.

Twitching a smile, Dahlgren said, "Something else you might keep in mind—a captain's authority isn't always worth striving for. Ever hear the expression, 'Careful what you wish for'?"

"Yes, Captain."

"Well, be careful, Andy. Be good and goddamn careful."

Stiffening, Tyler said, "I believe, when the time comes, I'll be up to the job, sir."

"So do I." Dahlgren grinned lopsidedly; his eyes were circled, even (it seemed to Tyler) haunted. "The difference of opinion, between us, Andy, is when that time'll be."

Again, Tyler said nothing; the moment was turning very awkward. He just wanted to go, get back to his work.

But the Skipper said, "Take this little jaunt, for

instance. We have a U-boat adrift in the good ol' Atlantic. Aboard it's a Smith-Corona-lookin' piece of junk that I'm told is a valuable coding device. Our job is simple: steal the son of a bitch."

Tyler smiled, just a little. "That 'simple' job does require a few nasty steps."

"Doesn't it, though? And there's the rub, Exec. This valuable piece of junk—how many lives is it worth?"

Tyler winced. "Sir?"

"How many men should I be willing to sacrifice to get Mr. Hirsch and Naval Intelligence their toy? Some? All? How about just Mazzola—he has kind of a smart mouth, kind of a pain in the ass sometimes. His mother may love him, but I don't, particularly. How about your buddy Emmett? He's kind of cocky, sometimes, don't you think? Dying would take him down a notch or two. Or that skinny kid in torpedoes, kinda keeps to himself . . . would we really miss him?"

"Sir, that's a hell of a way to look at it."

"Well, maybe this typewriter's worth *your* life? Do you think? Or mine, maybe?"

Tyler did not know what to say.

"You see, Andy, you hesitate. But a captain can't. He has to act. Otherwise, he puts the whole crew at risk."

"I'd die for any man on this ship."

"I know you would. Your bravery was never in question. These boys *like* you—a lot them look up to you like a big brother. Are you ready, are you willing, to lay their lives on the line?"

"I . . . I hadn't thought about it that way, sir."

"No, you haven't. You didn't have to. That's not part of what makes up an XO's job description. The skipper does have to think about, and deal with, such minor unpleasantries. He has to make decisions that men can die by and he can live with. It's not a science. You have to be able to make hard decisions based on imperfect information. Asking men to carry out orders that may result in their death, men who suffer the consequences when you've misjudged."

Tyler said nothing.

"If you're not prepared to make those hard decisions, without pause, without reflection, then you've got no business being a submarine captain."

Tyler, trying to absorb everything the Captain had flung at him, somehow managed to ask, "Then . . . what *is* the answer, sir?"

"The answer?"

"How many men *is* it worth?"

"Why, however many it takes, Andy." Dahlgren shook his head. "Ain't that a pisser? Tell Mr. Hirsch I'd like a word with him, would you, Lieutenant?"

And the Skipper returned to writing in the log, and Tyler went to get Mr. Hirsch.

Under the red lights of night running, supper was served in the tiny wardroom. The green baize table used for card games and briefings had been covered with a soft pad and a white linen cloth, and arrayed with fine china and silverware. Crowded around the elegantly set little table were Captain Dahlgren, Pete Emmett, Keith Larson, Lieutenant Hirsch, Major Coonan, and Andy Tyler. All but the Skipper wore uniforms of the Kriegsmarine, which heightened the surreal mood Tyler had felt all day.

Mess steward Eddie Green ladled oyster stew into their bowls from a tureen whose contents shifted with the pitch and roll of the ship in these rough waters.

"Sure wish I was goin' with you gentlemens," the mess steward said. "Sure there ain't room for one more at this rent party?"

"Sorry, Eddie," Major Coonan said. "We're fresh out of Nazi uniforms."

"Too bad, Major. I would make one badass stormtrooper, lemme tell ya—I would mess them Heinies over somethin' fierce."

"No question, Eddie," Dahlgren said, without irony, "they're missin' a bet not takin' you along."

That made Green smile, as he hauled the tureen back off toward the galley.

The Skipper eyed his Nazi-garbed companions, smiled, shook his head, and raised his water glass. "Gentlemen, despite your taste in dining apparel, I'd like to propose a toast. To the officers and crew of the S-33—and to our distinguished guests."

Coonan and even Hirsch smiled a little at that, pleased that some sense of respect had come their way, in the days of preparation for the mission. They raised their water glasses, as did every other man at the little table.

"May God speed you on this mission," Dahlgren said, with a somber smile, "and help us all speed the just end of this war."

"Here! Here!" more than one of them said, and Pete Emmett said, "Amen."

Glasses clinked; they drank.

They were just finishing their oyster stew when a Nazi-attired Wentz approached tentatively, his uneasiness apparent. "Captain, sir—the Chief says we're nearing the Chop Line."

"Very well," Dahlgren said. He turned to Larson, saying, "Ensign?"

Dahlgren rose and Lars followed him.

"And I need to get back to the radio shack," Hirsch said, standing, and he went out, Major Coonan trailing after, nodding good-byes.

That left Tyler and his friend Pete Emmett alone at the table.

Emmett produced a cigar, with his patented magicianly flourish, offered it to his friend and Tyler accepted it. A match materialized, and Emmett helped Tyler light up.

"This isn't going to explode, is it?" Tyler asked.

"The cigar or the mission?"

"Please." Tyler puffed; the cigar tip glowed orangely. "Aren't you having one?"

"Naw. My stomach's on the fritz."

Indeed Emmett had barely touched his soup.

"Maybe I shouldn't smoke this, then," Tyler said, not really wanting the thing in the first place.

"No, no, I'm fine." Emmett grinned. "Remember that gunner's mate, from our first patrol?"

"Oh, you mean Weisser?"

"Yeah, him. Son of a buck was immune to seasickness. I mean, a night like this, boat pitchin' and rollin'? Hell, he'd just laugh at us, for skippin' our meals, yellin' 'Lotsa chow for Tom, tonight! No competition! Lotsa damn chow!' "

Tyler laughed, enjoying the taste of the cigar. "Guy was a lunatic. Nice lunatic . . ."

"But a lunatic. Hell, any normal gob gets seasick once in a while."

But Tyler knew Emmett was not seasick. Pete had what Tyler had—precombat butterflies—and they both knew it.

Emmett plucked the German officer's cap from in front of him on the table, snugged it on at a raffish tilt. "I musta missed Pretend-You're-a-Nazi day at sub school."

"I think I missed that day, too," Tyler said. He flicked the German medals on Emmett's lapel and they jangled a little. "So—what are yours for?"

"This one's for banging Hitler's daughter. This was for delivering Himmler a new truss. Oh, and this, this was for finding Goebbels a choirboy who wouldn't talk."

Tyler grinned; damn Pete could always get a smile out of him.

"You think we're up to it?" Emmett asked.

"The mission?"

"It's just . . . What's it gonna be like, lookin' them in the eye? The Jerries, I mean. I know how to track 'em, fire at 'em, sink 'em . . . but that's from thousands of yards away."

Tyler sighed, nodding. "Close quarters combat, hand to hand . . . our boys don't know what they're getting into."

"Hell, Andy, neither do we. I'm don't mind tell-

ing you—I'm scared. All I can think about is
home."

"That's normal enough."

Emmett brightened. "Ever meet my folks?"

"Sure. Back at Annapolis."

"Graduation! Right! It's their anniversary tonight."

"No kiddin'?"

Emmett nodded. "If we hadn't put out to sea so
damn early, I'd be with 'em right now. Celebra-
tin'—no seasick stomach, no sir, putting away the
champagne and the expensive chow."

"How long they been together?"

"Thirty-five years—can you buy that? My mom
must be a saint for puttin' up with that cantanker-
ous son of a bitch. My pop, I mean."

"I gathered."

"What a great goddamn guy. I'd kiss the ugly
bastard on his lips if he was here right now."

"You'll see 'em soon enough."

"If I don't . . . if you see 'em first, I mean . . ."

"Come on, Pete, lay off."

"On the level, Andy. I know you can't tell 'em
about the mission, the top secret typewriter and
everything . . . but a lot of guys in this war buy it
for nothin'. Ammo dump blows up or something,
you know. Or on a sub, some damn malfunction
and you go down below and get crushed like a
damn pillbox."

"Stop this talk, Pete."

"Hey, it's the military, Andy. Situation Normal,
All Fucked Up? If I should happen to buy it, you'll
tell 'em, won't you?"

"What, that you love 'em?"

"Hell, they know that. That this was *about* something. An important mission. They'd want to know that."

"Sure thing. One condition, though."

"Yeah?"

"That you'll tell my folks the same thing."

"Sure! But I won't ask you to tell all my girl-friends. There's too many of 'em, and they'll all be too broke up."

"Yeah, well," Tyler said, "stay away from my girls, too. There's a fleet of 'em you'd have to talk to, and after bein' with me, you'd be such a big . . . *small* disappointment."

Then Eddie Green was there, dismayed by the largely empty table, wondering if anybody wanted strawberries.

"No thanks, Eddie," Tyler said, stubbing out his cigar.

"How 'bout you, Mr. Emmett?"

"Eddie, save me a bowl for when I get back."

"Yes, sir, Mr. Emmett." The mess steward began to clear the table. "I think you fellas is gonna work up a hell of a appetite, t'night."

"Eddie," Emmett said, "I think we just may." He turned to Tyler, rising. "Time for all good little Nazis to head for the Control Room, in case we're needed. By the way"—Emmett reached out and flicked Tyler's Nazi medals—"What are yours for, Andy?"

"Well, this one's for Hitler's *other* daughter. You know—the good-lookin' one, without the mustache?"

Heading down the passageway, the two college pals grinned at each other; for a moment, they might have been considering some campus prank, not the deadly mission that lay ahead.

On the bridge, Tyler knew, lookouts would be searching the waters through binoculars, helped by the weather, which had eased off into a persistent but mild drizzle. Searching, too, would be a small, recently installed radar dish, rotating slowly, sending information down to the radio room.

There, with surgical precision, Lieutenant Hirsch, attended by Radioman Wentz—both in German uniforms—operated the knobs on a device with a circular display and a needle sweeping over its glowing green face. To Wentz this gizmo was like something out of Buck Rogers.

They had been at this for a long time, with no results.

Still, Wentz found such advanced technology utterly fascinating.

And now a blip appeared toward the top of the circular display. Hirsch touched the pulsing dot, as if it were a religious object, offering healing powers.

"That's her, Mr. Wentz," Hirsch said, oozing self-satisfaction, pasty complexion blushing green from the display. "That's our U-boat."

Tyler was in the Control Room plotting on a navigational chart the S-33 in relation to the estimated position of the U-boat, when Hirsch appeared with the news.

"Let's get that radar antenna pulled off before it

attracts attention," a bright-eyed Hirsch said to Dahlgren.

"We're that close?" Dahlgren asked.

"We're that close. Radar contact at zero seven zero, range approximately ten miles."

Nodding, Tyler grabbed the receiver off the sound-powered phone, and repeated Hirsch's news to the Captain, adding, "Present course zero six zero, recommend shifting to zero seven zero."

Soon—raingear covering their Nazi uniforms— Tyler, Hirsch, Emmett, Larson, Trigger and Rabbit were on the bridge, the last two peering into their binoculars through the drizzle. The sea seemed calm, as the S-33 sliced through it; but the mood on the bridge was tense. The only sounds were the muted hum of the diesels and the lap of gentle waves.

Hirsch hoisted a signal lamp, aiming it dead ahead, as if the prow of the sub were a compass needle he was obeying.

The lamp made its *klik-klik-klik, klik-klik-klik, klik-klik-klik.*

And they waited.

Nothing—no response, out on what seemed, through the night and the drizzle, an empty sea.

Hirsch tried again: *klik-klik-klik, klik-klik-klik, klik-klik-klik.*

When the Naval Reserve lieutenant paused again, Trigger wiped beads of drizzle off his binoculars and scanned the horizon slowly. Then the boy stiffened.

"Signal lamp, sir," Trigger said, "on the starboard bow!"

Then they could all see it—distant light blinks, like fireflies in the wet night.

Emmett was already leaning into the voice tube, calling, "Enemy submarine sighted, starboard bow! Man battle stations! Captain to the bridge! *Captain to the bridge!*"

WITH THE EXCEPTION of Ensign Larson, whose duties would keep him in the Control Room until the last moment, the entire boarding party—thirteen of the seven men per raft—assembled in the crew's mess, squeezing around the shining steel tables like weirdly dressed waiters, their oilskin trench coats over full Kriegsmarine uniforms, their weapons under the oilskins. Faces were blank but nerves were jumping, as Chief Klough was threading through them, straightening collars, tugging coats down over handguns, smoothing uniforms like a fussy mother readying her daughter for the prom.

Coonan faced them, and gave them a smile that in no way softened his well-chiseled features dominated by the strong cleft chin and hard tiny eyes.

"Time has come, gentlemen," he said.

Tyler had to admit this broad-shouldered jarhead had done a hell of job, under impossible conditions, getting these men ready. Little actual combat training had been undertaken, mostly tactical pep talks, but this man who Tyler had dismissed as a prick had turned out to be a strong, fair-minded soldier who inspired confidence in himself and instilled confidence in his men.

"Remember," Coonan said with a nod to Tyler, "Lieutenant Tyler's raft has the conning tower and everything aft. My raft gets the gun crew. We have the advantage here—they aren't expecting a firefight. Just keep your heads, and keep your sense of geography—it's drizzling out there, nice and misty, and that helps us. Prevents the Krauts from getting a good look. Any questions?"

Head shakes signaled negative. The men barely glanced at each other. The tension was tight as a stretched garrote.

"Most important thing, gentlemen—no one shoots till I shoot." And Coonan lifted his Reising submachine gun, three ammo magazines electrical-taped together. "Do you read me?"

The men said, "Yessir," quiet but intense.

"You're good men. I'm proud to know you and serve with you." Coonan grinned. "You're not Marines, but you'll do."

That eased the tension just a bit—a bit—as a few tiny smiles blossomed.

Then Coonan's smile disappeared and so did theirs. "Okay, then. We have a surprise party to throw. Lock and load."

And they did, the *krik-krak* of weapons cocking echoing in the steel-walled mess, absurdly like the sound of Rice Krispies getting milk poured on.

Tyler, catching his own reflection in the polished steel surface of a table, saw a frightened face staring back. That would not do. Dahlgren's lecture fresh in his mind, Tyler did his best to bury his anxiety under a clench-jawed blankness.

Coonan was tucking his Reising under the trench coat. The men were doing the same with their weapons when he said, "Hold up," and he went around checking each man's gun, giving every one of them a small moment, a look, a word.

Tyler thought: *Leadership. That's leadership.*

To the boyish Trigger, youngest man in the group, Coonan said, "Watch Mr. Tyler's back for me, son. Countin' on ya."

Trigger brightened. "Yes, sir."

"You'll be all right, son. We're all gonna do just fine. Lieutenant Tyler, if you'll come with me."

Tyler followed Coonan up to the Control Room, Coonan stepping inside, Tyler waiting in the passageway just outside the open hatchway. Larson, in full German uniform, no oilskin raincoat yet, was waiting with a position slip for Dahlgren, who was coming down the ladder from the bridge.

"Captain," Larson said, handing Dahlgren the slip, "I calculated this by giving the resupply sub a fourteen-knot speed of advance."

"Good," Dahlgren said, heading to the periscope. "That's a prudent estimate. Where does your latest plot put that resupply sub?"

"Twelve hours away, sir."

"Excellent. Mr. Larson, you've done everything that could be done aboard ship. Time for you to join the boarding party."

"Yes, sir. Thank you, sir."

"And Mr. Larson?"

"Yes, sir?"

"Give them hell. And pass that word along."

"Yes, sir."

As Larson slipped past him, Coonan stepped forward. "Boarding party ready, Captain."

"Good. I'm trusting you to watch out for my boys."

"You can count on me, sir. They'll be men when they return."

Dahlgren twitched a non-smile. "I've put the 33 low in the water, Major. I want to give that damn U-boat as little silhouette as absolutely possible."

Coonan smiled tightly, nodding. "Outstanding, sir."

Dahlgren reached for the intercom mike, and into it said, "Gun crew topside! Prepare to disembark the boarding party." He clicked off and turned back to Coonan. "One thing, Major."

"Yes?"

"This shindig starts to go to shit, I will blow that fucking Nazi tub right out of the water, Enigma or no Enigma. Am I understood?"

"Loud and clear, sir."

The two men shook hands, and traded nods.

Moving past Tyler, Coonan said, "Report to your captain and join me aft."

Tyler said, "Yes, sir," and then he poked his head into Control and said, "Confirming that we're all set, sir."

Dahlgren came over to him and leaned against the bulkhead. "You heard what I said to Coonan— this goes to hell, I'm bagging that bastard."

"Yes, sir."

"All right. You go get 'em their goddamn typewriter, Andy, then get the hell out."

"That's the idea, sir."

Dahlgren's eyes tensed. "Are you all right?"

"Does it show, sir?"

Almost whispering, the Skipper said, "I don't think anybody but me could see it. Listen—the boys are going to do fine."

"I know they will, sir."

"We talked about sacrifice, earlier."

"Yes?"

"We learn to live with that. But we like it when nobody on our side dies."

"I can't promise you that, sir."

"I know you can't. But we have to try. That experience you need to get, between now and when you're ready to skipper your boat . . . you may well get it in the next hour. Good luck, Andy."

And Dahlgren extended his hand.

Tyler took it, and the handclasp was firm and warm; so was the expression in the Skipper's eyes.

"Godspeed, Skipper," Tyler said, and headed back aft.

On the bridge of the U-571, Kapitanlieutnant Gunthar Wassner, in a good mood, watched through his Zeiss binoculars what he thought were German sailors moving about the deck of what he had every reason to believe was the German resupply sub they'd been anxiously awaiting. Though a full moon cast a shimmering ivory sheen on the sea, visibility was poor, the drizzle insistent, forming a hazy curtain between the two submarines as they drifted one hundred yards apart in eerily calm waters.

Through the binoculars, Wassner observed as sailors removed inflatable rafts from storage containers, bringing up boxes and sacks of provisions from below. Then, from the bridge of the resupply sub, came the yellowish blinks of a signal light.

Reading the message, Wassner—a smile nesting in his beard—lowered his glasses, and leaned into his speaker tube, to address a crew badly in need of good cheer: "Our comrades have brought fresh eggs and bananas. And even better than food, they have brought our mail!"

Wassner could hear the cheers from the Control Room below, and the boys on deck had heard him, too, and were equally gleeful. His men had been through hell; how nice it was to hear from home, to be reminded of who they were besides sailors, to remember why they were out here enduring such lonely, perilous duty.

On the aft deck of the S-33, bags of equipment waiting, two rafts were inflated by CO_2 tanks with one, then another, *whoosh*, and lowered quickly into the gently lapping, drizzle-flecked waters. The moonlight was like fog you see through, though the drizzle was less forgiving.

Walking the slats of the deck, Coonan directed and prodded the work, speaking occasionally, but very softly, knowing that if words of English were to travel across the waters to that surfaced Nazi sub, this party would be over before it began.

Along with the rest of the boarding party, Tyler—exchanging a brief look with Pete Emmett that said nothing and everything—helped load the supply sacks down into the rafts, which the gentle waters made an easier task than it might have been, the inflatables bobbing only ever so slightly.

Still, the sponginess of climbing aboard was disconcerting, if not quite alarming, though soon the two rafts were fully loaded with people, as well, and they had begun traversing the endless hundred yards between subs.

Even with the moonlight, it was a forbidding dark expanse of water, and the officers and sailors of the S-33, playing commando, wore anxiety-etched expressions. So did Lieutenant Hirsch. Only Coonan seemed to have the cool, battle-hardened visage the situation required.

Aboard Tyler's inflatable, Tank and Mazzola were seated midraft, doing the rowing, with Emmett and Trigger and Peterson behind them, and Tyler and Hirsch up front. Aboard Coonan's inflatable, doing the rowing, were Rabbit and that quiet skinny kid from the torpedo crew whose nickname was Fats, with the Chief, Larson and Griggs in back; at the bow, Coonan and Wentz. A German speaker up front, in either case.

Tyler again worked at forcing the anxiety off his face, clenching his jaw, his .45 automatic in his right hand, against his leg, under his trenchcoat. Every man was armed under the oilskin coats, and more weapons lurked in their cargo—the bags of tools and supplies at their feet.

Next to Tyler, Hirsch—so businesslike and condescending in the preparation stage of this mission—was shaking so bad, the raft was shaking with him. And the reserve lieutenant's pistol was showing, Hirsch thumbing the safety nervously.

Hating to speak at all, knowing English meant death, Tyler whispered, "Tuck that away."

Hirsch did, but the trembling even worsened, as if the man had been seized by Saint Vitus' dance.

So softly he was barely audible, Tyler said, "Relax—we're almost there. We're gonna bushwhack these bastards good."

Hirsch drew in a deep breath, nodded, swallowed, nodded again and seemed to ease some. A little, anyway.

In Coonan's boat, his mouth barely moving, like a deft ventriloquist, the Marine major was whispering, too, giving his crew a rundown: "Twelve topside. Four in the bridge, with mounted machine gun, flak gun. Three foredeck. Five aft."

The major had a trained eye. To the others, little of what he reported was discernible. Under ideal conditions, a surfaced sub was difficult to spot, so little protruding above water that its outline could easily avoid detection, just the flatness of the deck with the rise of the conning tower.

But as the two rafts neared the German sub, not only it but the mist-shrouded figures on its bridge and deck became distinct. An oilskin-slickered man who must be the captain was watching through binoculars, much as Dahlgren no doubt was doing from the bridge of the S-33; lookouts were slowly scanning the spitting skies for Allied aircraft. Only a single lookout was watching the approaching rafts.

And that oilskin-slickered character who was probably the captain.

The only sounds were those of the gently lapping sea, the gulping strokes of paddles, the radio-interference-like hiss of drizzle. Finally the light conversation of German sailors cut through these few sounds, as the U-boat loomed ahead of them, no longer an abstract shape in the night, but a battered, black-iron reality.

The boarding party in the inflatables could clearly see the German sailors waiting on deck, eager to greet them, anxious for fruit and letters from home and mechanics to repair the wounded whale they lived in.

Waiting, that is, with MP-40 machine pistols in hand.

"Jesus H. Christ," Tank whispered behind Tyler.

"Steady, gentlemen," Tyler whispered back. "Wait for the signal."

Sailors carrying machine guns was something that hadn't been anticipated. Coonan had advised them that U-boat sailors were not prone to infighting, that they never risked a gunfight unless the odds were on their side. Suddenly that statement seemed to Tyler to ring with a different resonance.

Now they were very close. The U-boat yawned like a dark wall before them, above them not just vague moving sailor-shapes in the misty night, but sailors, real men, with real guns.

So softly he himself could barely hear it, Tyler whispered, "Say something, Mr. Hirsch."

But the German-speaking Naval Reserve lieutenant had a glazed, frozen expression. At least the son of a bitch wasn't shaking anymore.

"Mr. Hirsch," Tyler whispered.

"Hello the boat, asshole," Mazzola hissed.

"Shut up," Tyler whispered back.

Every English word a death sentence, if heard.

A German officer—the chief electrician, though the Americans couldn't know that—yelled out cheerfully in his native tongue, "Ahoy, repair crew! Welcome! Do we have a job for you!"

Tyler glared at Hirsch, who looked as if he'd had a stroke, eyes glassy and unblinking behind the drizzle-dotted wireframes, marbles stuck in his putty mask of a face.

"Goddamnit," Tyler whispered, "say something."

The chief electrician called down again. "Which of you are mechanics? You better be good!"

White-knuckling the .45 under the trenchcoat, Tyler—wishing he could understand and speak the gutteral garbage that was German—darted a look toward the other raft, hoping Coonan would pick up on the fact that Hirsch was screwing the pooch.

Coonan did, and shot a look at the man beside him, Wentz, the boarding party's other German speaker.

Wentz nodded, and began to improvise. "We're all mechanics!" he called up to them.

Hearing Wentz speak German sent a wave of relief through Tyler.

"We're all very skilled," Wentz said, voice cracking a little, but doing well, "and we should have you under way by sunup!"

This interchange in German seemed to snap

Hirsch out of his spell. Shouting—a little too loud—he managed, in German, "Ahoy!"

Tyler gave him a "settle down" look, and Hirsch nodded, picking up a bogus mailbag, lifting it up like a fish he'd caught. More German flowed from Hirsch, more easily now, naturally. "Anyone up there want this filth? Our captain ordered us to get rid of these naughty notes and indiscreet pictures, reeking of French perfume!"

Up on deck, the German sailors were laughing and cheering, even whooping with delight.

Pleased by this response, Hirsch continued, wild-eyed, "Who wants this sack of soiled purity? Or should I sink it in the ocean?"

Tyler, who knew the gist of what Hirsch was saying, from their briefings, also gathered the gist of the response of the sailors, dancing around up on deck, saying, "No, please, no!", "You do, we'll throw you in after!", and "My girl is different, she's a nice German girl!"

Then the chief electrician tossed a line to Tyler, and the raft was pulled alongside; as Coonan's raft neared the conning tower, a sailor tossed them a line, as well.

Suddenly Tyler found himself looking up at a grinning young German face and a hand extending itself his way. Hesitating, for just an instant, allowing the bizarre reality of the moment to pass, Tyler took the hand, and allowed himself to be pulled onto the slats of the deck of the German U-boat.

"Welcome, sir," the chief electrician said. "Are any of you from Weisbadden?"

A friendly enough question, and certainly an innocent one; but Tyler didn't understand a word of it, spoken in German as it had been.

He risked grunting a non-response, then, thank God, Hirsch—still down in the raft, alongside the boat—came to his rescue, saying, "I'm sorry, none of us hail from there."

On the bridge, Captain Wassner did something unusual for him, particularly in front of his crew: he laughed.

It was so delightful to see his sailors, ecstatic, dancing on the deck, trading good-natured barbs with the supply officer bringing them their mail. How wonderful it was to see them having such a great time, anticipating these missives from home, and from Occupied France, where they had forged special relationships.

Rather idly, suspecting nothing, Wassner glanced at the two rafts. First, the one where the chief electrician had just helped an officer on deck. Then, the one near the conning tower, which was just being tied up. He gazed down at the trench-coated officers and sailors in the inflatables. One of the faces looking up at him from the raft had a strangely tight expression. Why was that sailor glaring at him, anyway?

Then Wassner caught the glint of something—a weapon in that sailor's hand, just snaking out from under the oilskin of his coat!

The captain of the U-571 shouted, "Alarm! Repel boarders!"

And someone opened fire.

TYLER HAD THE .45 out before the startled chief electrician had time to react to the burst of gunfire, aft, Coonan standing in the inflatable and letting rip with the Reising submachine gun. At the deck gun, just forward of the conning tower, in back of where the chief electrician stood greeting what he thought was a supply officer, three German sailors manning the deck cannon took Coonan's barrage of bullets, the slugs dancing across them at a terrible 45-degree angle, puncturing their oilskin rain gear, shaking them like naughty children and tossing them overboard in a puffy mist of scarlet.

Up on the bridge the lookout at the MG-34 was swinging the big belt-fed machine gun around, nose tilting down for a better shot at the inflatable from which Wentz and the others had yet to climb aboard.

"Down!" Tyler yelled, hitting the deck, literally, and the MG-34 fragmented the night with its relentless rapid fire, its first victim an unintended one, the German chief electrician, whose body went flying overboard in bloody pieces, one moment the man standing above him, the next nothing left but the flecks of blood on Tyler, who lay on the algae-slick slats of the wooden deck over the sub's steel hull.

Overwhelmed by the bullets zipping inches over his head, Tyler, .45 in hand, shot a look at his raft just as the skinny kid called Fats got cut in half by the machine-gun fire, falling overboard in two pieces, making two splashes, as everyone else in the inflatable ducked. Then, despite the bullets whizzing, keeping Tyler flat on the wooden deck, the boarding party of his raft clambered up onto the deck, keeping low, opening fire as they came.

He could hear gunfire from Coonan's raft as well, the night shattered by the single cracks of handguns, the rapid rumble of machine guns, muzzle flashes like fireworks in the misty darkness. As his men joined him, Tyler got to his feet, looking toward the conning tower, catching sight of Peterson getting shot, dead, and falling back into Coonan's raft, the others climbing aboard, however, their weapons knocking Germans off their lookout perches like pins in a shooting gallery, including that flak gunner on the MG-34, a surviving lookout ducking behind the bridge coaming, where bullets zinged and dinged.

Then the lookout popped back up, a machine-gun pistol in hand, hurling its *rat-ta-ta-ta-tat* at Tyler and his men; they scattered, rolling on the narrow deck, the wood getting chewed up, and Tyler, on the tumble, fired upward.

The lookout pitched from his perch, slid down

the side of the sub into the sea, which swallowed him, and his damn machine gun.

Tyler looked toward the conning tower, which husky Griggs—part of Coonan's unit—was already scaling, a Thompson in one hand.

"Careful who you shoot!" Tyler yelled to his men, in a momentary lull of gunfire, reminding them that both teams in this ballgame were suited up in the same uniforms.

Then the crack of a handgun sent Griggs back over the bridge coaming, toppling down onto the deck, landing hard, near the unmanned MG-34, making a terrible gurgling sound, clutching his neck.

Gasping as if the wound were his own, Tyler ran to him.

On the bridge, Captain Wassner—his boys shot to ribbons all around him, either draped over the deck and bridge, or tossed bleeding to the merciless seas—had just been ducking down the hatch when the big American (and they were Americans, not British, he could tell from their shouts and commands) came climbing over the coaming with teeth bared and a submachine gun in one hand.

Wassner had met this fearsome sight calmly, firing his Luger, drilling the boy through his throat.

As the invader toppled back over the bridge coaming, Wassner descended the ladder into the conning tower, stopping only to close the hatch, then moving past the young frightened helmsman, his face as round and white as those of the many gauges around him.

"Hold onto that hatch," Wassner told the helmsman, "keep them out!" knowing he'd left the boy a hopeless task, then stepping down the ladder through the second hatch, closing it behind him, dropping into the Control Room.

Wassner was met by the startled wide-eyed faces of his young Control Room crew all around him, seeking answers he didn't have. Then the dreadful chatter of a machine gun, whinging and dinging and singing off the metal of the conning tower above, told its dreadful story: the young helmsman hadn't been able to hold off the invaders long.

"Grab onto that hatch," Wassner commanded his two planesmen, "and hold fast!"

They scrambled up the ladder and held onto the hatch, held it fast as their captain had commanded, hanging from the wheel-like handle like boys swinging from tree limbs.

"Good job!" Wassner said, then turned to the remainder of his crew. "Dive, dive, dive! We'll drown them like the goddamn rats they are!"

As the young men flew to their stations, into the Control Room rushed Kohl, Wassner's fresh-faced exec, carrying a handful of ordnance, God bless him. Soon the boys were tearing the greasepaper wrappers off like starving beggars after bread, and then six gleaming Schmeisser MP-40s were cradled in a dozen hands.

Kohl was handing out clips, and these too were eagerly unwrapped. Above them the two boys, hanging onto the hatch, were swaying, as if a sudden breeze had blown through the long, narrow ship.

But it was only the invaders, above, struggling to twist open that hatch.

Moments before, on the deck of the U-571, Tyler had been leaning next to Griggs, his fellow native of the Lone Star state, looking into the agonized face, touching the dying boy's cheek. Around him, the men from his inflatable were scaling the ladder onto the conning tower.

Then Coonan was at Tyler's side, bending down. "He's dead. The living need you more."

Somehow Tyler got to his feet and followed Coonan up the ladder onto the bridge; the night was silent now, the firefight out here, over—any further action would be down inside this man-made beast.

The twelve survivors of the boarding party were crammed onto the bridge, and the massive Tank was crouched over the closed hatch, trying to twist that wheel handle open, putting every ounce of his brute strength into the effort.

Which quickly paid off.

Open just an inch, but that inch was enough for Rabbit to ram the barrel of his Thompson in, and down, and let rip with half a clip that sent bullets zinging in the compartment below, ricocheting like crazy within the tower. Someone down there yelped in pain.

Then Rabbit withdrew the snout of the submachine gun and silence followed, just a moment of it, after which Coonan said, "Anybody in that conning tower is ventilated. Open it, Tank."

Tank did. There was no resistance.

Tank, Rabbit, Coonan and Tyler descended the

ladder into the gore-spattered iron room of the conning tower, and somehow fitted themselves into the ten-by-twelve space, cut by the polished steel pipe of the periscope tube. The sounding gear, navigational and fire-control gauges were little different from on their own sub.

"Okay, Tank," Coonan said, yanking the shredded body of a young German helmsman off the hatch, "pop the cap on this beer bottle."

And the burly machinist mate straddled the hatch wheel and locked on his huge fists and twisted, veins in his forehead popping, cords in his neck standing out. He grunted, he groaned, he grimaced, but he budged it.

Again, just an inch.

Just enough for Rabbit to cram in the nose of that tommy gun and blast away.

No sooner had the machine pistols been passed around and clips inserted than submachine gun fire was echoing through the Control Room, lead raining down from the snout of a Thompson, bullets pinging and zinging off metal.

Wassner dove for cover, behind the chart table, his captain's cap flying.

First to die were the two brave boys who'd been hanging onto that hatch wheel, ripped apart, arms shot off, human beings exploded into scraps of meat, scattered on the deck below.

Then the hatch snapped open.

Wassner sat up, training his Luger up at the open hatch and the gore-dripping ladder the invaders would come down—only, instead, a grenade dropped in, clunking to the deck, and Wassner covered himself, curled against the bulkhead, thinking he was moments from death, even as a high-pitched alarmed American voice above spoke the English words, "You're gonna blow us all up!"

But the explosion was all sound and fury, no shrapnel, just smoke, and terrible noise, a stun grenade stirring confusion and providing cover for the invaders.

The first to jump down, a huge American with a submachine gun in his hands, was met by two of Wassner's boys dazedly trying to raise their Schmeissers to fire. But they were too disoriented from the stun grenade, bleeding from their noses and eyes, and then—when the brutish American let a burst go from the machine gun—were bleeding from newly drilled orifices, as well, tumbling to the deck, dead before they hit.

Keeping low, Wassner couldn't get a bead on the big American, and was angling around the periscope to do so as two more invaders dropped down, the first one as small as the brute was large, the other a dark-haired, dark-eyed youth. Both had Thompson submachine guns.

Wassner had the dark-haired one lined up in his Luger's sights . . .

. . . but his exec, Kohl, got a shot off first, and another shot for good measure, taking the dark young American down in a twisting, moaning pile!

The other two invaders, the brute and the small one, howled in rage and unleashed their Thompsons on Kohl and the exec went down in a shuddering dance, bleeding from dozens of wounds.

Kohl had barely hit the deck, dead or dying, when two more Americans dropped down in, a skinny handsome one and a thirtyish cleft-chinned character who had combat experience in his hard eyes, and a Reising submachine gun in his hands.

And Wassner suddenly found himself with only two of his boys left alive, facing five machine guns, albeit one of them held by the wounded dark-haired invader who was himself sprawled on the floor, blinking in pain.

With a heavy sigh, Wassner raised his hands in surrender; and the other two sailors did the same.

The cleft-chin American curled a lip at them and motioned for them to lie down, and Wassner did, his two remaining boys following his lead, but so quickly it may not have looked that way to the Americans.

Wassner watched, helplessly, as the skinny American sprayed machine gun fire through the forward door, and another dark-haired American, a husky Italian-looking one, dropped into the Control Room and hit the deck running, moving to the after door and spraying his Thompson as if he were a fireman hosing a fire. The cries of boys getting hit by those bullets made Wassner wince.

Then a smaller, older American dropped down the hatch and just as the Italian was reloading sent another burst of bullets through the after door, eliciting more yowls and wails of pain and terror. At the forward compartment, the handsome skinny American was slamming a new magazine into his Thompson while the small invader picked up the

slack, blasting machine gun fire down the passageway.

The boys on his boat were dying, and there was
nothing he, their captain, could do.

But as he lay on the cold deck, Wassner noticed—amid the blood-leaking bodies—his captain's hat, where it had flown, clear across the
Control Room.

The Americans did not know he was the captain.

And he was not about to tell them.

Tyler, at Coonan's command, had stayed at the
back of the line with the two German speakers,
Hirsch and Wentz, and the young inexperienced
Trigger. When he heard Coonan below yelling,
"Stern team go!" he knew it was time to join the
fray.

The first of the trio to drop into the crowded
Control Room—where Tank, Rabbit, Larson,
Coonan, Emmett, Mazzola and Klough had preceded them—Tyler was startled by the harrowing
sight of the blood-splashed bulkheads and deck, the
bodies of the Germans scattered, some in pieces.
Even though he'd heard the gunfire above, nothing
could prepare him for the hell he'd just plunged
into.

Mazzola, Tank and the Chief were moving into
the passageway, ducking through the round portals,
heading aft, tommy guns at the ready.

"Bow team, go!" Coonan was saying.

Then Tyler noticed Lars, in a fetal ball of pain
on the deck, and rushed to his side, knelt by his

friend, who looked up in fear and panic and yet said, "Andy, I'm okay! Go!"

Tommy guns in hand, Pete Emmett and Rabbit were already moving forward, and Wentz and Hirsch followed. Coonan was part of that team, too, but the Marine major was hovering over three captive German sailors, one in an oilskin topcoat not unlike theirs, the other two in fatigues.

Coonan was thrusting out a black-billed white captain's cap.

"One of you birds lose this? One of you ugly fuckers the captain, maybe?" He kicked the trench-coated one. "What about you, Adolf? You the Herr Kapitan?"

The prisoners apparently didn't understand Coonan, or were pretending not to, not even looking at him or the accusing cap.

Young Trigger, Thompson in hand, finally dropped down into the Control Room, his eyes widening at the sight of the bloodshed.

Almost casually, Coonan—finishing up a quick but thorough frisk of the captives—said, "Trigger, guard these bums. Anybody moves, live up to your nickname."

"Yes, sir."

Coonan nodded to Tyler and the two men moved forward, leaving Trigger and the fallen Larson to guard the prisoners.

They caught up with the others just through the first round portal, a compartment shared by the radio room, the captain's tiny stateroom, and the bunks and nook of the wardroom that represented the sub's officers' quarters.

Tyler paused at the radio room—which looked ransacked, obviously quickly stripped of its papers by its fleeing overseer—where Hirsch hovered over a pedestrian-looking pine-cased typewriter sitting innocently on the counter with a wall of radio gear behind it.

All the fuss, all the shooting, all the death, was for this: the Enigma code machine.

But Hirsch did not look happy; in fact, he seemed dismayed. "Cover's open," he said. "Rotors have been removed."

"Rotors?" Tyler asked.

"The heart and soul of this machine. Without them, it really is just a damn typewriter. We've *got* to find them."

"After we secure the ship," Coonan said, pointedly.

And Hirsch, frowning, nodded. "The codebooks are gone, too. They're almost as important as the goddamn rotors. Shit. Wentz, write down the equipment settings—that's a start, anyway. And police up every scrap of paper in here."

Wentz nodded, and began going through what little remained in the radio room. He plucked two disks from the counter.

"Got something here."

Hirsch, momentarily excited, said, "What?"

"No—it's nothing."

"What?"

"Billie Holiday. Bing Crosby."

Frustrated, disgusted, Hirsch reached for the typewriter-like machine, with both hands, when Coonan grasped his arm.

"Let me check it," Coonan said.

Hirsch frowned in confusion.

"For booby traps," the major added.

The reserve lieutenant's hands drew back, as if the Enigma were the burner of a hot stove.

Following a nod from Coonan, Tyler joined Emmett and Rabbit up ahead, Pete on the left, the little torpedoman at the right, moving forward cautiously, with the unenviable, terrifying task of pausing at curtained bunks, yanking them back with a *snik*, Thompsons at the ready if some German had taken refuge within.

Stepping over the occasional corpse, human refuse flung rudely in the passageway, the ghastly litter of warfare, Tyler—.45 in hand—drew back a curtain on a bunk, and a wide-eyed blond sailor aimed a pistol at him.

Tyler dropped to one knee, as the bullet flew over his head, the sound of the gunshot deafeningly loud, and he fired upward, his weapon making an even louder noise, punching a deadly hole in the young sailor's chest, driving him back against the wall as if the bullet were a nail.

Rising, Tyler—a sick bile churning in his stomach—looked with horror and disgust at what he'd done, the young sailor slumped there empty-eyed in the bunk, the red-black stain on the blouse of his fatigues spreading like the blossoming of a terrible flower.

Swallowing, Tyler shut the curtain, and turned to see Emmett and Rabbit looking his way, with wide, alarmed eyes. Coonan, Hirsch and Wentz, down the passageway by the radio room, were also staring at him.

"Clear," Tyler said, and swallowed. "All clear."

Emmett came over to him. The Sinatra-handsome chief engineer had a haunted look. "You okay, Andy?"

"Guess now we know."

"Huh?"

"What it's like lookin' 'em in the eye."

Elsewhere on the ship, aft, Chief Klough followed Mazzola and Tank through the crew quarters, with open bunks—nowhere to hide—and some hammocks, which the men prodded with their machine-gun snouts, getting no reaction. Between the bunks was a table, still bedecked with dirty dishes, and Klough half crouched, to peek under it.

The son of a bitch came flying out from there, swinging a meat cleaver, a German bulldog in fatigues and an apron.

The blade swished past the Chief's ear, and he swung the Thompson around and slammed the butt into the side of his assailant's head. The stocky little guy fell like a poleaxed mule, the cleaver clanging to the deck.

"Looks like the cook," Klough said, trying not to show how hard he was breathing.

"Yeah," Mazzola said. "Bet the boys on this tub didn't criticize his chow, much."

They moved through the tiny galley and the Chief held up a hand at the round portal leading into the diesel engine room. Then the grizzled chief petty officer dove through and rolled and came up with his tommy gun at the ready.

No sign of anything, here in this nest of pipes and handwheels and funnels and levers, the big diesel engines still, their pistons frozen, hatch to the engine room closed. The smell of oil and diesel fumes dwelled, but nothing, no one, else.

Klough and Tank moved to the far left and right of the engines, along the hull, as Mazzola stalked down the middle, machine guns poised. Soon they determined the engine room was clear, and the closed hatch—a door, not the usual round portal—awaited them.

Klough stepped forward, but Mazzola held up a hand. "If you don't mind, Chief."

"Be my guest."

Mazzola nodded to Tank to open the hatch, which Tank did, and, teeth bared, eyes wild, Thompson ready, Mazzola threw himself inside.

A long moment passed.

"Come on in, boys," Mazzola said, and Klough and Tank stepped through and joined him.

A dozen German sailors—hands up, looking scared shitless—had surrendered.

"There's a new sheriff in town, fellas," Mazzola told the prisoners, as Klough counted heads. "You're in my territory now, and this here tommy gun's the law."

The sailors exchanged confused, frightened expressions. Klough almost felt sorry for them—they were kids, scared kids, playing war, just like the babies of the S-33 that he looked after.

But Mazzola was smirking at their fear, saying, "What a buncha pansies."

The cocky kid had a lot to learn—if he lived long enough to learn it.

Then Klough stuck his head through the hatchway and called down the passageway: "After compartment's secure! Bringing out twelve!"

Duckwalking, Tyler and Emmett were making their way through the baroque underground workshop of the forward torpedo room, with its loading rails along the ceiling, gleaming chains of pulleys, suspended torpedoes, walls lined with mattresses of berths designed to swing down at bedtime. They moved slowly along, cautiously, Rabbit tagging after.

"We've got some deck plates open," Tyler said, gesturing ahead with the .45 in hand.

"Careful," Emmett said. "They could be hiding down in the bilge—"

As proof of Pete's wisdom, a German sailor popped up, like a jack-in-the-box, dripping bilgewater, squeezing the trigger on his Schmeisser.

And Tyler, the lead man, would have been dead, but the German sailor—dealing with an unfamiliar weapon handed him in this emergency—had not cocked his weapon.

Stunned, horrified by the instant awareness of how close he'd come to death, Tyler blasted off three rounds from the .45, three echoing reports that were like thunder in the metal room, jostling the startled sailor, who dropped back down in the square hole in the floor with a pitiful turd-in-the-toilet-bowl splash.

Keeping back a few feet, Tyler, Emmett and Rabbit crowded around the space where the deck plates had been pushed aside, and from the space the shot-up sailor had sunk back into, a pair of hands—empty hands—poked up in surrender.

"Don't shoot!" the sailor cried in German.

Not understanding, Tyler said, "Get up out of there, goddamnit, or I'll blow your fucking head off!"

"Get out!" Emmett yelled. "Or he'll kill you!"

The sailor—a different one, a hydrophone operator on the U-571, though of course the Americans could not know that—began to crawl out, soaked from the waist down.

Emmett pulled him the rest of the way out, roughly, like a big catch onto the deck of a fishing boat, and patted him down for weapons, telling Rabbit, "Get down in that bilge and check for a scuttling charge. And watch your ass, or it might get blown up in your face!"

"Yes, sir," Rabbit said, and hopped down into the bilge with a splash. Soon he had hauled a canvas bag up onto the deck, a knapsack sort of affair, filthy with bilgewater.

"Check inside," Tyler said. "But look for trip wires, booby traps, first!"

Rabbit was careful, but this was no satchel charge. Books and papers spilled out.

"Damn!" Tyler said, examining them, "we got the codebooks! Confidential papers, God knows what else. Mr. Hirsch. *Mr. Hirsch!*"

Hirsch came on the run, just as Emmett was having a look at the codebooks and papers, which had spilled out amid much foul dirty bilgewater.

"Andy," Emmett was saying, "the damn ink is running!"

"Those things are water-soluble!" Hirsch cried out, like a worried mother. "Dry them off, quick!"

"Blankets off those bunks," Tyler said, and he and Emmett scrambled after some, and within moments were patting the books and papers dry.

In the meantime, Coonan had entered and was giving the hydrophone operator a more thorough frisk, going through his pockets, his boots, everything but stripping the poor bastard.

Rabbit stood up in the hole where the deck plates had been removed. "No explosives down here, that I can see."

Hirsch strode over and, his face tight, said, "Sailor, listen to me carefully, this is vital—check for four disks about the size of canning jar lids."

"Yes, sir," Rabbit said, and went back down into the bilge.

Hirsch knelt over the frightened German and demanded, in German, "Where did you hide the rotors?"

"What rotors?" the sailor answered, seeming almost relieved to be asked a question in his own language.

"The Enigma rotors! Where are they?"

The hydrophone operator—who of course knew exactly what Hirsch meant—shrugged, and then said nothing more.

Coonan hauled the German to his feet and

dragged him out. Hirsch paced while the sounds of splashing, like a child in a tub, indicated Rabbit's search in the bilge continued.

And Andy Tyler and Pete Emmett—after a raid that Annapolis had in no way prepared them for—stood looking at each other, relieved to be alive, each relieved his best friend was still alive, both knowing that the carnage they had witnessed—and helped dispense—had changed them forever.

THE MIST HAD escalated into rain, as the transfer of prisoners and plunder got under way, the darkness before dawn cracking and crackling with occasional lightning, the sky shaking with real thunder, not the man-made warfare variety. The S-33 and the U-571 were side by side now, a mere fifteen yards apart, like two surfaced whales getting to know each other, basking in the gloom and the rain.

Lieutenant Commander Michael A. Dahlgren, on the bridge of the S-33, observed and directed the proceedings taking place at the aft decks of the two subs, involving three inflatable rafts, one of which was a survivor of the raid.

It had been a long night for the captain of the old S-boat, mostly spent up here on the bridge; watching and hearing, from a hundred-yard distance, the flickering fireworks of the battle between the two rafts and the German sub had been a stomach-churning hell for Dahlgren—observing at a terrible remove the storming of the sub, watching through his binoculars as if witnessing some play or movie, wondering which of his boys were winning posthumous medals.

Now, in the aftermath, he felt almost guilty at his sense of relief knowing only two men had been lost; and already, in some compartment of his mind, he was composing very different letters to two families, so that they would know their sons had not just been cannon fodder to their captain, but distinct individuals whose singularity had not been lost on him.

With a tiny ironic smile, Dahlgren gazed down at the aft deck of the S-33 as shambling, stunned German prisoners, who'd been ferried from their own sub by an inflatable, were met by the astounding sight of a Negro sailor.

As the German sailors stood on the deck planking, Mess Steward Green was giving them mock-friendly, how-you-doin' greetings, as he used a grease pencil to number each of their foreheads, a nicely dehumanizing touch, Dahlgren thought, for the master race—although seeing them relatively close up, Dahlgren could tell the enemy sub's crew was a mostly youthful one, making his kids look like seasoned sailors.

"Der Führer ain't gonna be pleased with you boys for lettin' that sub slip through your fingers," Green was saying, as he grease-penciled another forehead. Another gob was at Green's side, giving the prisoners a thorough frisking, like a veterinarian checking mutts for ticks. "Lucky thirteen! Next!"

Dahlgren called across the rain-dancing water to Trigger, on the bridge of the German sub. "Tell Mr. Coonan to shake a leg! Sunup in an hour."

"Yes, sir!"

Down on the aft deck of the U-571, Dahlgren could see Chief Klough strapping the wounded, semi-conscious Larson onto a stretcher. Dahlgren could make out everything they were saying, in part due to the water carrying the conversation to him, in part because Larson was damn near screaming, not so much in pain as in confusion and shame.

"Get out of this rain, Chief!" Larson was saying, delirious. "Catch your death! Catch your death!"

"No cold's gonna catch me, sir," Klough told him. "Now you just relax."

"I'm all screwed up, everything's screwed up!"

"Easy, Ensign. Gonna be all right—got some nice morphine for ya over on the 33—"

"I didn't even get a round off, Chief! Didn't even get a round off. What about my wife, Chief? What will Peggy think?"

"She's gonna be real glad to see you. You got the million-dollar wound, Ensign. You're goin' home."

A lightning crack punctuated the Chief's sentence.

Then two gobs helped Klough ease Larson— whose babbling had ceased, for now anyway—into the inflatable alongside the sub, for the short journey home to the S-33.

As lightning flashed outside, Tyler moved through the Control Room of the German submarine where similar if smaller electrical flashes were momentarily illuminating the gauges, pipes, ducts and valves of the nerve center of this boat, whose designation, they now knew, was U-571.

Tyler's pal Pete Emmett was taking flash picture after flash picture, like an enthusiastic tourist, screwing one fresh bulb after another in his camera's flashgun, already on his second roll of thirty-six 35mm exposures. In fact, at Hirsch's command, Emmett was taking this rare opportunity to record the controls of the enemy sub, which was, after all, due to be scuttled any moment now. Only Emmett's photos would remain to provide key information about the layout and interworkings of a German U-boat—an intelligence windfall to rival that of the Enigma code machine itself.

Moving through the hatchway past the radio room, Tyler encountered the vaguely tasteless sight of sailors ransacking the sub for anything of importance. Of course, the ongoing search for the Enigma rotor disks alone justified this looting, but when Tyler came upon Mazzola—at the very bunk where Tyler had shot the blond sailor, who'd been hiding there, and lay there still—enough was enough.

Mazzola was stuffing French postcards into the pockets of his oilskin trench coat, which didn't bother Tyler, really—what gob wouldn't grab up nudie photos of mademoiselles? But when the Brooklyn boy began pulling a gold ring off the finger of the blond corpse, that tore it.

"Leave the poor bastard's wedding ring alone," Tyler said.

The ring was off now, in Mazzola's hand. His handsome face contorted as he said, "Aw, what the hell's the harm, sir? We're dumpin' the bodies in the drink, ain't we?"

"I killed him," Tyler said. "It's my call."

"Yes, sir."

Tyler held his hand out and Mazzola sighed and put the ring in the officer's palm.

"Now check out the head," Tyler told Mazzola, who shuffled off to the nearby toilet, just outside the hatchway to the bow torpedo room.

Then Tyler, drawing a deep breath, saying a silent prayer for himself and his victim, slipped the ring back on the stiffening hand of the sailor who had tried to kill him.

"Nothing in here but shit, sir," Mazzola called, holding the door of the cubicle with one hand and his nose with the other. "Pretty rank shit, at that!"

Mazzola stepped aside as Tyler had a look for himself. The crapper was full, all right.

"Don't these German pigs know how to flush?" Mazzola asked.

Frowning in thought, as well at the smell, Tyler said, "My hunch is, they do . . . usually."

Tyler had a look around the foul-smelling cubicle. A small cabinet provided newspaper strips that served as toilet paper. A metal hook was some kind of plumbing device. Tyler grasped it and plunged it in the unflushed bowl, poking around, hitting something that was not feces.

When the hook came back, it had snagged a small silver disk.

"That's no turd," Mazzola said, impressed.

"I believe it's an Enigma rotor," Tyler said.

"No shit?"

"Actually, in addition to shit . . ."

In the engine room, aft, Major Matthew Coonan, USMC, was taping bricks of TNT to the big seawater pipes used to cool the diesels. With him was Machinist Mate Charles Clemens, known to his pals as Tank, the burly brute who had so impressed the major in the raid.

"You got cast-iron balls, son," Coonan said, stabbing in a detonator connected to an M2 igniter and a long length of waterproof fuse. "You shoulda been a Marine."

"Wish we had these babies on the 33." Tank was inspecting the huge diesels, lovingly touching pipes and fiddling with valves like a man in foreplay with a beautiful woman.

"Unclog your ears, grease monkey," Coonan said. "When you hear me yell to ya, pull this pin. Got it?"

"That pin, yes, sir."

"Then haul ass out the after hatch and leave it open. Ten minutes later, this boat goes ka-blooey."

"These beautiful engines and all?"

"Every Kraut one of 'em."

Tyler hustled into the Control Room with his plumbing hook dripping slime and bearing four silver rotor disks through their spindle holes.

Hirsch and Wentz—in the process of wrapping the Enigma machine (enclosed in its pine box) with an oilskin overcoat, ready to secure it with twine—

looked up at the grinning Tyler, first alerted to his presence by the smell.

"Wash 'em off, and they're all yours, Mr. Hirsch," Tyler said.

"Mr. Tyler," Hirsch said, with what could only be described as a shiteating grin, "you're the man of the hour."

As Hirsch said this, Major Coonan was just slipping through the hatchway into the Control Room, and his eyes lit up at the sight of the muck-dripping rotors. He smirked and shook his head. "Well done, Mr. Tyler, well done! And you thought you had crappy assignments before. . . ."

Hirsch took the hook with the rotors off Tyler's hands, rushing out to get the disks cleaned off, as Coonan sidled over to the Exec and said, "You found those babies just in time, Mr. Tyler."

"You rigged the boat with a scuttling charge?"

"I did. Your man Tank is back there. Hope he's smarter than he looks."

"He'd about have to be, wouldn't he?"

Coonan grinned, patted Tyler's shoulder. "You did a hell of job, Tyler. I'd take you along on any raid, any time."

"Kind of you to say, but, uh, I'd just as soon you Marines recruit from within, next time around."

"Understood."

Soon Tyler was on the aft deck, where the transfer of prisoners and spoils was winding down. The rain was steady, but the thunder and lightning had faded.

He gave Hirsch a hand with the bulky twine-tied, oilskin-wrapped Enigma machine, passing the thing down to Coonan, in an inflatable. The major put the precious package midraft, then turned and accepted a wrapped bundle of papers from Wentz.

Chief was on deck, and Emmett, his newsman-style flash camera in hand, was climbing down the conning-tower ladder from the bridge. Shortly they would be leaving the U-571 behind, to await Coonan's scuttling charge.

Feeling an eerie sense of calm, an abiding relief that the nightmares of this night would soon be over, Tyler stepped back and watched as Trigger piloted a raft in which two sailors rowed toward the S-33 carrying the last batch of prisoners, two boys and an older, bearded sailor; and he waved and smiled at the barely conscious Lars, on his stretcher, in another inflatable, which two sailors paddled. Lars even managed a smile in return.

Coonan, too, was surveying the scene, his raft the only one that hadn't pushed off; Tyler would be riding with him, as would the Chief, Emmett, Wentz, Hirsch, Mazzola and Tank.

"*Now*, Tank!" Coonan called.

Moments later, Tank came scrambling out of the aft hatch, yelling, "Fuse is burning, sir!"

"Ten minutes, ladies!" Coonan said. "Let's get boarded!"

Emmett said, "Hey, Andy! Hold it right there. Got a perfect shot of you, with the S-33 in the background."

Tyler, kneeling to hand a few last items to Coonan in the raft, glanced up, and saw that Emmett had strolled down the aft deck, and was screwing in a fresh flashbulb.

"I thought you were taking recon photos," Tyler said.

"Come on, gentlemen," Coonan said, "move it along!"

"I think the Navy owes us one exposure," Emmett said, with half a grin, lifting the camera, poised for a shot. "Say cheese."

On the bridge of the S-33, Lieutenant Commander Mike Dahlgren, glancing away from the transfer of men and materiel between the two parked subs, looking out at the vast empty darkness of the sea, noticed something stirring in those endless waters, a glittering phosphorescence coming right his way. . . .

As Pete Emmett took the flash photo of his friend Andy Tyler, something happened that seemed, for a crazy instant, to have been a result of the camera's click. But there was no connection; this just another absurd moment in the brutal absurdity of war.

And Tyler didn't even see it, just heard the deafening blast, felt the shock waves that threw him to the deck, as the submarine exploded.

Not the U-571, with its TNT charges, no: *the S-33!*

The torpedo—which Dahlgren had seen coming but not soon enough even to speak a warning into the tube on the bridge—must have hit damn near dead center, because in the sudden dawn of the explosion, bodies were sent spinning through the air, falling, splashing, into a sea instantly littered with burning debris. The broken shape of the S-33 was consumed with massive columns of flame, as steel and men and fragments thereof went flying in every direction, petals cast off the billowing blossom of orange and yellow.

Tyler did not see much of it, shielding himself from the blast, face down, clutching the slats of the seesawing deck. For this he might well have counted himself lucky, not having to witness a hatch from the S-33, whirling through the air like an iron discus, decapitate his friend Pete Emmett.

Tyler also missed seeing Major Coonan get hit with a chunk of flying fiery shrapnel, sinking into his chest like a huge medal he'd rather not have received, living just long enough to stare down with disbelief at the thing that killed him, then slumping forward in the raft.

Nor was Tyler subjected to the sight of Ensign Keith Larson, who'd been blasted out of the inflatable, strapped to his stretcher, sinking, slowly sinking, yelling, "No, God, please, no," in what was part prayer, part curse, until water filled his mouth and the waves took him down.

And he did not see Trigger's raft, punctured by flying metal, rocked by it, sending Trigger and the three German POWs toppling overboard, the two sailors who'd been rowing going down with the inflatable, having been struck instantly dead by the shower of shrapnel.

When he finally risked pushing up from the deck, Tyler saw crewmen jumping from the burning wreck that had been the S-33—even shackled German prisoners were leaping in, taking their chances in the water with its patches of burning oil.

And he saw Pete Emmett's camera, broken and blood-spattered, on the deck—Emmett's body had followed his head into the sea.

Staggering through this nightmare, the sky orange with flame, black with smoke, the sea thrashing with sailors struggling to stay afloat, Tyler felt his mouth moving but no words seemed to come out.

Finally he heard someone yelling, "Everyone, belowdecks! It's an attack!"

His voice, he realized suddenly; *he* was saying it.

But no one was responding to his command. Mazzola, Klough, Wentz, Rabbit—they were standing on the deck of the German sub, looking toward the flame-spouting shell of S-33, frozen there, horrified, mystified spectators at a ghastly show.

Then another explosion, a smaller one, rocked what little remained of the S-33; this seemed to break the spell and suddenly the sailors on the aft deck of the U-571 rushed to the aid of friends flailing in the water nearby—the Chief tossing a line to Trigger, pulling him in, Mazzola running to help the effort.

But Tyler knew that more torpedoes were damn near certainly on their way, and there was no time for this.

He yelled, "Everyone below! Now! Chief! Take her down!"

Wentz and Rabbit were scrambling up the conning tower, as Mazzola and Chief were hauling Trigger onto the deck.

Somebody yelled, "The Enigma!"

Hirsch, of course.

Frantically, the Naval Reserve lieutenant was pointing to the raft in which the dead Coonan seemed still to be guarding, and floating away with, the oilskin-wrapped code machine.

Tyler jumped into the water, the freezing cold a shock to a system that had already endured its share of shocks in one night; but he managed to grab onto the raft and swim with it, haul it, quickly guide it back to the U-571 where Hirsch reached down and plucked out the Engima, set it dripping on the deck—then gave Tyler a hand, pulling him back on board.

Standing nearby, Tank was pointing. "I see the Skipper!"

Several sailors, including a handful of Germans, Eddie and other familiar faces, were simply too far away from the deck for a rescue line to do any good. One of these faces belonged to Captain Dahlgren.

"Damn," Tyler said softly.

Dahlgren was thrashing weakly, trying desperately to stay afloat, head bleeding—and then his hand raised, waving them back.

"Go. . . . Dive. . . ." The voice was feeble, barely audible, yet commanding as hell.

The Exec's eyes met those of his imperiled captain and Dahlgren's expression said: *No hesitation, Andy. No second thoughts.*

"Belowdecks now!" Tyler yelled, heading for the conning tower. Tank was scrambling for the after hatch, closing it after himself, Hirsch, Mazzola, and

Klough climbing to the bridge ahead of Tyler, disappearing below.

From the bridge he looked out at Dahlgren, gave his friend and captain a quick salute, and descended into the enemy ship, where even now Tank was defusing the TNT charges, turning the floating bomb of the U-571 back into a boat.

Tyler was spared the sight of his captain, strength fading, clutching a chunk of floating debris, turning his back on the U-571, rolling over to watch his dying submarine, its carcass engulfed in flames and smoke, a fire the boat quenched itself, when finally its bow rose with a sad, strange regal nobility, slipping silently into the sea.

10

TYLER YANKED THE hatch shut between conning tower and Control Room, and dogged it, twisted its wheel good and tight, and slid down the ladder into the heart of the German boat.

Around him his men—like him, attired in German Navy uniforms—were hastily doing their best to find the U-571 equivalent of their tasks on the S-33, moving swiftly but not panicking. The only one who looked truly shell-shocked was Hirsch, tucking the Enigma machine beneath the chart table like a schoolboy hiding his dirty magazines under the bed.

Tyler took a deep breath, steeling himself—and in a few seconds, a complex series of thoughts flew through his mind.

This was a sub like any sub—open the required vents, set the planes for angle of dive, switch on electric motors, and she would go down, driven by motors and fins, the increasing weight of ballast tanks aiding the descent. Simple science, simple math.

And this Control Room was like any Control

Room in any sub—steering equipment, flood valves, drain pumps, periscope, instruments and controls for every system. The boat might be foreign, but the atmosphere, and the machinery, were the same, in fact *had to be* the same.

That a deadly, bloody firefight had taken place in this small chamber less than two hours before was a distant memory, the enemy dead having been unceremoniously dumped in the sea; and the Chief had thoughtfully wiped the room down, cleaning it of the spatter of gore, prior to the search of the sub for the Enigma and other key materials.

The S-33 was gone. Obliterated. This was their boat now, the U-571 was *his* sub, now—and that a German boat would be home to his first command was an irony that did not elude Tyler, even in the controlled frenzy around him.

And controlled it was: a fundamental rule of submarining was not to scream when trouble came, but to deal with it coolly.

"Chief!" Tyler said. Not a shout or yell, just raising his voice to be heard. "You find the vents?"

"Everything's in goddamn German," Klough said, touching gauges and controls lightly, a sighted man trying to read Braille.

The two German speakers aboard—Hirsch and Wentz—would be key to their success, their survival.

"Wentz!" Tyler said, eyes searching among the dials and gauges for the intercom microphone. "The vents! Trigger, take the helm."

"Yes, sir."

"Mazzola, the planes."

"Aye, aye, sir."

Trigger and Mazzola took their respective stations and began tentatively testing the controls.

Snatching the intercom mike off its overhead perch, Tyler sent his voice echoing through the ship. "Tank, I need speed and I need it now—get those screws turning! Lights are on, so there's juice left in the batteries, some anyway. Rabbit, find out how many fish we've got in those tubes, and then figure out how the hell to launch 'em."

From the shell-like spout of a speaking tube came Tank's reply: "I'm on the E-motor control panel, sir, but I can't read this shit! And you know what a short life *valve-turners* lead!"

"Hold on, Tank—don't go experimenting." Tyler turned to Hirsch, the only man in the Control Room not doing anything. "Rear torpedo room, Lieutenant, now—translate for Tank."

Looking nervous but obviously glad to help, Hirsch nodded and ducked through the round hatch and rushed down the passageway, aft.

Their other translator, Wentz, was at the Chief's side, Klough tracing a pipe to a large red overhead valve, saying, "What's this big one, here?"

Wentz shook his head, frustrated. "Hell if I know, bastard's not labeled . . . but Chief, I think these right here are the aft ballast tank vents. Yes, they are!"

The Chief flew to where Wentz was pointing at valve wheels over the aft doors. "Then the ones up forward gotta be the forward vents," Klough said, wincing in thought.

Reaching for levers overhead, Wentz said, "And

I got the midships valves! And here's the induction valves—"

"Make sure they're shut," Klough said firmly. "Don't open those vents till I know for sure we ain't got a hole in this tub. Where's the fuckin' Christmas Tree?"

Tyler had been searching for the damn thing, and now stood before a panel of lights and multiple valves and hand wheels. "Is this it? Wentz, is this the Christmas tree? Says here, *klar, klar, klar*. Can we dive?"

"*Klar* means clear," Wentz affirmed. "Each compartment shows clear. It's gotta be, yes, sir—look at those white lights—we got a white greenboard, looks like."

"Go ahead, Chief!" Tyler called. "Pop those vents!"

And Klough opened the forward vents, as Wentz did the same with the middle and aft vent valves, Klough finishing first and pitching in to help Wentz, as the familiar, reassuring roar of air out of tanks confirmed they were on the right track.

Smiles blossomed around the Control Room, as the U-boat began to submerge, leaving behind a surface scattered with burning patches of fuel.

The new crew of the U-571 was unaware that another sub was submerging as well, or the charred shell of one, anyway. The remains of their previous duty station—that relic of another war, the S-33— were sinking rapidly, only the forward section lingering above water, almost vertical, outstretched like the arm of a drowning man.

At the last moment, the forward hatch opened

with a billow of smoke, and a badly burned, blinded sailor tried pitifully to claw his way out, tumbling back in as water poured into the hatch, to drown in darkness.

Then the waves swallowed the S-33, providing the dead ship a final resting place, just as the U-571 was seeking a different sort of salvation in these same waters.

"This is the forward trim," Wentz was telling the Chief, translating, pointing to this and to that, "aft trim, auxiliaries. Here's suction, discharge. This one says 'to sea.' "

"Got it," Klough said.

Despite the tension, Tyler was starting to feel at home, figuring out, and making sense of, the speed, depth, course, control surface indicators and other gauges all around him.

"Passing fifteen meters," Mazzola said, from his bench at the planes.

"Recommend shutting the main vents!" Klough said.

"Shut main vents," Tyler said.

Starting aft and working his way forward, the Chief rose and closed the three main vents.

"Wentz," Tyler said to the radioman, "get in the sound room and put your ears to work. We need to know just what the hell is out there."

"Aye, sir!"

As Wentz stooped through the hatch, moving into the nearby hydrophone nook, Tyler said, "Depth twenty meters."

"Depth twenty meters, aye, sir," Mazzola said.

"Chief, take the dive."

"I have the dive," Klough said. "Mr. Mazzola, bow planes on zero, control your depth with stern planes."

"Bow planes on zero, control depth with stern planes, aye."

"Rabbit," Tyler said into the intercom mike, "I need a report!"

Mazzola said, "At twenty meters."

From the speaking tube came Tank's voice: "All ahead full, sir! Batteries are flat and draining fast."

Tyler could have guessed that, from the flickering lights in the Control Room.

Wentz called out from the hydrophone shack, "Mr. Tyler, I hear a ship breaking up!"

Tyler twitched a half-frown. "The 33."

Everyone in the Control Room flinched at the thought, but shook it off—there would be time for reflection, for mourning, only if they lived through their own ordeal.

Wentz said, "Wait . . . wait! I hold a submerged sub, at zero one zero. Close, sir, damn close—less than a thousand yards."

"It's that goddamn resupply sub," Tyler said, spitting the words.

"It was their torpedo that got the 33," the Chief said.

Tyler asked, "Trigger, what heading are we on?"

"Two eight zero, sir!" Trigger stood at the secondary steering position here in the Control Room (the first position was in the conning tower, unmanned at present).

"Right full rudder," Tyler said. "Steady on zero one zero."

"Aye, aye, sir," Trigger said, fingers on the rudder buttons, "right full rudder, steady on course zero one zero."

Into the intercom mike, Tyler said, "Tank! Starboard back full. Rabbit—still waiting for that report!"

From the tube came Tank's voice: "Starboard back full, aye, sir."

Klough said, "Watch your depth, Mazzola, or the ship will squat like it's shitting."

"Aye, Chief."

Tyler said through his teeth into the intercom mike, "Rabbit—any time!"

Finally the speaking tube brought Rabbit's voice to the Control Room. "We got four fish, sir. Tubes are flooded, but I can't open the muzzle doors till I equalize. And I can't do that, 'cause I can't read this damn gibberish!"

Tyler said, "Understood." He called to Wentz in the hydrophone shack. "Wentz! Go forward, help Rabbit."

But Wentz leaned out of the shack, one ear covered by the black antennaed cup of the headset; he was frowning. "Sir, enemy submarine close aboard. Torpedo in the water! Torpedo in the water!"

"Belay my order, Wentz, stay where you are," Tyler said, getting back on the mike, his eyes on the compass, begging it to turn. "Hirsch, hightail it to the bow torpedo room!"

Moments later Hirsch was tearing through the Control Room, on his way to help Rabbit, as the compass began gradually to turn.

"Trigger," Tyler said, "mark your head every ten degrees."

"Aye, sir. Passing three two zero."

They could feel the boat slowly turning to starboard. . . .

In the bow torpedo room, Hirsch was met by a jumpy Rabbit, ushering him in, saying, "What's what in this nuthouse? I can't equalize these tubes. You gotta find the fuckin' shutters and muzzle doors, equalizing valves. . . ."

Hirsch quickly scanned labels, and asked, "Could this be it? 'Pressure differential?' "

"Yeah, yeah, yes, hell, yes!" And Rabbit began spinning handwheels. "Help me open these babies!"

And Hirsch joined in.

In the Control Room, the compass needle was swinging faster—just not fast enough. Tyler watched it, praying, perspiration beading down his forehead; he wiped the moisture off with the back of his hand—his eyes were bleary enough without the salty sting of sweat in them.

"Come on," Tyler said softly.

"Passing zero zero zero," Trigger said.

"Come on, baby, come on . . . swing, you bastard, swing around. . . ."

Wentz said, "Closing on us, sir."

And they could hear it, growing ever louder, churning toward them, close as hell, an underwater lawn mower screaming through the sea . . .

. . . and then the sound dropped off, as it streaked past the sub, barely missing her spinning screws.

"Torpedo missed," Wentz said, beautifully redundant words.

Relief flowed through the Control Room . . .

. . . short-lived.

"Two more fish in the water!" Wentz said. "Best bearing to that U-boat: zero degrees."

"Helm, check your swing," Tyler said. "Steady on course!"

"Aye, sir," Trigger said.

"Chief, stand by, ready to flood forward trim."

Klough scurried to the aft trim valves.

"Rabbit," Tyler said into the mike, "get ready to fire a spread. Tubes one and two! Zero gyro! Fire!"

Tyler waited—nothing.

"Rabbit, fire!" he said into the mike.

In the bow torpedo room, Hirsch was hurriedly pointing, saying to a confused Rabbit, "Push that!"

And both Rabbit and Hirsch hit the firing valves.

The torpedoes were hot, sending off an eardrum-popping screech—which would have been fine, had they not been staying put in their tubes.

Hirsch and Rabbit, eyes wide, ears ringing as the torpedoes continued their hysterical shrieking, exchanged panicky glances.

In the Control Room, Tyler and everyone else looked around in alarm as the piercing vibration reverberated through the boat.

Grabbing the intercom mike, Tyler said, "What the hell's going on?"

"Hot run!" came Rabbit's voice out of the speaking tube, barely audible over the torpedo squeal. "Fish're stuck! I musta missed an interlock or something!"

"Get them the hell out of there, Rabbit," Tyler

said into the mike, "before we sink our damn selves!"

In the bow torpedo room, Rabbit was frantically trying every valve he could find, asking Hirsch, "You see anything says, 'firing air'? 'Impulse air'? Anything like that?"

Head moving back and forth, as if watching a frenzied tennis match, Hirsch kept scanning labels, then, suddenly, forcefully, thrust a finger and said, "That!"

And Rabbit pulled the levers, hit the firing valves, and with a pair of satisfying echoing *ka-thunks*, the torpedoes ejected!

Into the speaking tube, Rabbit said, "One and two away! Lining up tubes three and four."

From the intercom, Tyler's voice said, "Fire tubes three and four!"

This time a *ka-thunk* preceded the screech, and then another *ka-thunk* and another screech, as one, two more torpedoes fired—perfectly—the bow of the U-571 belching air as four deadly fish now swam toward their target.

And both Rabbit and Hirsch heaved sighs of relief, and leaned against each other, exhausted.

In the Control Room, Tyler paced, biting his lip.

"All fish running hot," Wentz said from the hydrophone shack, "straight and normal."

Tyler counted to himself. If Wentz was correct about the U-boat's position, the two subs would be facing each other, right now, like a couple of Old West gunfighters. And the other pistolero in this shootout was no doubt taking his best shot, too . . .

"Torpedoes in the water!" Wentz said, confirming Tyler's suspicion. The radioman winced, listening carefully, so carefully. "They have us bracketed, sir!"

And they waited, as the torpedoes bore in on them, on both port and starboard. Again, came the churning, the whirring, but this time all around, seemingly coming from everywhere, the sound building to a terrible underwater scream. . . .

"Starboard torpedo missed, sir," Wentz said, and swallowed. "Well wide of starboard."

Tyler nodded curtly, still counting, listening for the U-571's own torpedoes hitting paydirt.

"Port torpedo closing, sir!" Wentz called, unnecessarily, as the underwater scream was in everyone's ears, announcing their visitor.

And now, suddenly, bizarrely, that scream turned into giant fingernails scratching down a monstrous blackboard.

Tyler clenched his fists, trying to keep his terror out of his face—the goddamn torpedo was scraping along the length of the ship!

Every wide-eyed face swiveled to port, as the grating talons clawed along the skin of the ship, as if the torpedo were toying them, playing with them. . . .

It went on forever—or was it fifteen seconds?

Either way, it stopped, and the goddamn thing did not explode, somehow it did not explode itself to fragments and them into chum, and Chief Klough—whose face was paler than a flounder's underbelly—was shaking his head, saying, "Well, that's a first, that's a goddamn fuckin' first. . . ."

Immense relief in his voice, Wentz called out,

"Missed us! Port torpedo off on its merry way, sir!"

Tyler swallowed, nodded, still counting to himself, as the Chief said, "What about ours? What are our fish up to?"

Every face was raised, expectant, except Tyler's, which stared at the deck, as he counted, counted, counted—until the numbers, the seconds, ran out on him . . . damn. Damn.

"I . . . I think they all missed, sir," Wentz said.

And though the crew of the U-571 could not know it, they had indeed missed, and badly, with their first three torpedoes—by dozens of yards. They were facing down a Type VII-C U-boat with camouflage markings, captained by a Wolf Pack veteran, manned by a seasoned crew, who were preparing another barrage of torpedoes for the hijacked German sub.

As if he knew all this, as if he was aware of how bad his odds were—and, in a way, he did—Tyler drew in a breath, let it out, reluctantly nodded, acknowledging their failure, and the crew members sighed, and shook their heads, hangdog expressions all around.

That was when the explosion rocked the waters and the ship and seemingly the entire world—and it was not *their* ship exploding, either: it was the U-boat, its conning tower taking the fourth torpedo dead center.

No cheers rang on the U-571, no hoots or hollers or handclaps. Tyler and his crew looked around at each other, shocked at their success, amazed to be alive, and, most of all, relieved—not to mention spent beyond belief.

Mazzola looked at Trigger, let out a sigh that must have started at his toes, and wiped the sweat from his brow with the sleeve of his Kriegsmarine uniform.

"Did I hear a sub blow up," Mazzola asked, "or did I just shit my pants?"

Nervous laughter broke the tension, or at least eased it.

Then Wentz called out, "The U-boat's breaking up, sir! I can hear the bulkheads bursting!"

No submariner could greet this news gleefully; they knew they had just delivered, to that enemy crew, the very fate they most feared for themselves.

Steadying himself against the periscope, Tyler felt dazed, hardly able to grasp the fact that the crew of the U-571 had survived—more than survived: they had prevailed.

"Mr. Tyler?" The Chief, at his handwheels, seemed poised for another order.

"Yes, Chief?"

"What about the 33, sir?"

The mention of their lost boat sent a palpable wave of melancholy through the Control Room; any small sense of joy, at their unlikely triumph, was expelled.

"You're right, Chief," Tyler said, nodding. "Take her up."

"Aye, sir," the Chief said, spinning handwheels, air hissing as if from a huge punctured tire.

"We'll pick up survivors," Tyler said, offhandedly.

Hoping there'd be some.

DAWN HAD YET to break and the wind had picked up, howling like a bored banshee, stirring waves, sending spitting, stinging rain directly into the faces of Tyler, the new captain of the U-571, and Trigger, the youngest sailor on the ship, as the pair stood on the bridge surveying a desolate, heart-breaking vista.

As Tyler scoured the waters with the bridge-mounted searchlight, this tableau of abject loss had been revealed in the streaky white glimpses provided by its beam: patches of burning oil boiling like festering scabs on the skin of the sea, debris from the S-33 drifting, as were a few survivors and several floating corpses.

Down on the aft deck, Chief Klough and Mazzola had spotted Eddie Green in a pass of Tyler's searchlight beam, and were tossing him a line. Tyler sighed and smiled, pleased that this one friend, at least, had made it. Soon the Chief and Mazzola had hauled the exhausted mess steward onto the deck, Rabbit stepping up to slip an arm around Green's waist and escorting him toward the conning tower.

As Green and Rabbit scaled the ladder and joined Tyler and Trigger on the bridge, Tyler clasped Green's hand.

"Mighty glad to see you, Mr. Tyler."

Rain flecked their faces, the wind howled as they spoke, waves lapping at the boat, sometimes rolling across the deck.

"I was afraid we were going to have to cook for ourselves, Eddie."

"Now that *is* a frightenin' thought. . . . Did the Skipper make it?"

"No."

"Lordy, Lord, that is a shame. God bless him. How . . . how many of us are there, Mr. Tyler?"

"Nine, Eddie."

"Ten countin' me?"

"Nine counting you, Eddie. I added you to the roster the moment I saw you."

Green managed a small smile. "You're gonna do fine, Mr. Tyler. You're gonna do the Skipper proud, I just know you are."

Tyler swallowed. "Thanks, Eddie. That means a hell of a lot."

Green nodded and grinned, though his eyes were sadder than hell, and Rabbit ushered the groggy mess steward down into the boat through the conning tower.

Reports from below were not encouraging. The lights had flickered, then faded entirely. Tank—who'd been tracing fuel lines, clicking on a flashlight to keep at work—sent word that the battery was indeed dead. Some of the radio gear was down,

Wentz had reported, though some limited communications would be possible.

A cry from the water made Tyler swing his searchlight around: "Help! Please! Help me!"

The voice, though speaking English, bore a telling accent.

Tyler could see, down on the aft deck, the Chief and Mazzola spotting the flailing survivor in the searchlight beam.

And he also saw Mazzola pull his Luger from the holster on the belt of his German naval uniform.

Flinching at what the impulsive Brooklynite seemed about to do, about to call down to him, Tyler was relieved by how the Chief handled the seaman, their conversation audible from Tyler's perch on the bridge.

The Chief simply placed a hand on the arm Mazzola had raised, as he'd taken aim at the German thrashing in the dark waters.

"Back off," Klough told him.

"Chief, he's a goddamn Nazi!"

"Yeah, but we aren't. Back the fuck off, sailor!"

And Mazzola reluctantly lowered his arm, glumly holstering his sidearm, as the Chief threw the survivor a line and began hauling the man in.

Beard dripping, drenched, frazzled, wearied, the German had a haggard look that emphasized his age; he was not a boy, like so many of the original crew of the U-571. He wore a yellow turtleneck sweater made gray by the sea, his brown trousers turned black, his heavy boots unlikely survivors of his watery plight. Standing slumped, hangdog, a singularly unformidable, even pitiable figure, he presented no indication that he was Kapitanlieutnant Gunthar Wassner, the captain of the U-571 returned from a watery grave.

"You speak English?" the Chief asked him.

Swallowing air, chest heaving, the slouching figure nodded. "Yes, yes. Ein little bisschen. Yes, yes."

"Frisk him," the Chief told Mazzola, who did, roughly, taking the man's watch, putting it on his own wrist.

From his perch on the bridge, Tyler had to smile, albeit wryly, at Mazzola's action—this was a step up, at least, from looting the dead. But Tyler's smile was fleeting—he was not pleased with the prospect of dealing with a prisoner, under these already harrowing conditions.

"Here," Mazzola said, handing Klough a cigarette lighter.

The Chief looked it over; no identifying marks. "What's your rank, Adolf?"

The bearded prisoner frowned, narrowing his eyes, shaking his head, apparently not understanding.

"What do you? What's your job?"

"Ah, *mein* job! *Elektriker*." The German mimed getting electrocuted, adding a comic, "*Zzzzzzttt! Elektriker*, yes?"

Smiling, Klough said, "Well, you're either an electrician or a clown—and we could use some electrical skills around here more than a good laugh. Maybe you can squeeze some juice out those batteries."

On the bridge, Tyler—still manning the searchlight—asked, "See anybody else out there, Trigger?"

"No, sir."

Could that really be all the survivors? Just Eddie and that damn German?

"Sir, *there's* someone!"

"Where?"

"There! It's . . . it's the Skipper."

And it was, limply draped over a chunk of charred wreckage, Dahlgren—his body—turning slowly, riding the choppy waves, like a surfer who had fallen asleep waiting for the big one.

Breath jerking with emotion, eyes damp with more than the stinging rain, Tyler leaned against the bridge rail, unable to take his eyes off his dead friend, his captain, caught in the searchlight beam.

Down on deck, the Chief saw the sad sight, too, the spotlight making a star out of Dahlgren in the drama of death and destruction played out on the oil-burning, debris- and corpse-scattered waters. Klough moved forward for a closer look, leaving Mazzola to tend to the prisoner.

To himself, Klough said, "Aw, hell," and in his mind and heart sent a farewell to his skipper and a prayer to his Lord.

Up on the bridge, Tyler clicked off the searchlight. "We've done all we can up here."

"Sir?"

And Tyler looked into the youngest face on the ship, a babyish mug filled with trust and hope and fear.

"What do we do next, sir?"

"Go below," Tyler said, knowing that that didn't really address the question the boy had asked.

In the wardroom of the U-571, just forward of the radio shack, the officers' mess table protruded sideways into the aisle; seated on a padded bench next to the curved wall were Chief Klough and Lieutenant Hirsch, each with a flashlight in hand—the lights on the boat off, thanks to the dead battery. This created an oddly eerie ambience, the darkness cut by the sharpness of the flash beams, which gave shadows to their faces, highlighting bone structure. Klough and Hirsch watched and provided illumination as Tyler, standing opposite them, smoothed out a map he'd found.

Pointing to the southwestern tip of England, Tyler said, "Land's End."

Hirsch was frowning, possibly from the dim light, possibly due to Tyler's suggestion. "Why there? Why not Newfoundland?"

"Except for Occupied France," Tyler said, with a shrug, "Land's End is the closest."

"Newfoundland would be a better choice," Klough said, "if we had the fuel."

"How much do we have?" Hirsch asked.

"Six tons," Tyler said.

"The Jerries weren't just waiting for food and mechanics," the Chief said, "they also needed refueling."

Still frowning, Hirsch asked the Chief, "Can we make it to England?"

"With nine men?" Klough rolled his eyes. "On

a boat built for fifty? Jesus, we don't even know if we can get the boat running."

"We'll get the boat running," Tyler said, but even he knew he didn't sound very sure of that.

"Okay, then," Hirsch said, his frown showing teeth now, "assuming we get this thing moving, who's in charge?"

Tyler flinched at this; perhaps it hadn't been intended as an insult, but he felt wounded, shocked that this would even come up.

"Navy regs say it's the senior seagoing officer," Klough said matter-of-factly, "which is Mr. Tyler. Now, Mr. Hirsch, I understand that you were, in tandem with the late Major Coonan, commanding the raid. But I doubt you feel qualified to captain this ship."

Hirsch nodded toward Tyler, looking to the Chief. "No offense meant to the Exec here, but it seems clear you have the most experience, Chief."

"That is true."

"And we're in an extraordinary situation, a small group of us on a commandeered enemy sub, in possession of materials that could change the course of the war. I believe we should do what's right."

"Mr. Tyler just saved all of our asses," the Chief said tightly, "guiding us through as narrow a scrape as I have ever survived. I would give him my vote, if that were necessary, Mr. Hirsch, and he sure as hell has my loyalty. But the only thing that counts here is Navy regs."

Hirsch drew in a breath, let it out, nodding grimly. "It's your command, Mr. Tyler."

Tyler, about to say that he didn't realize he

needed Hirsch's fucking approval, was stopped by the Chief talking first.

"Well, Mr. Tyler—I guess you got your boat."

And, despite the spirited defense Klough had given him, Tyler could hear the implication in the Chief's voice: *Let's hope you're up to it.*

Soon the Chief led Tyler and Hirsch into the Control Room, flashlights and lanterns here and there minimizing the darkness, if not the gloom. Cut, bloody, drained, the new crew of the U-571 was scattered about the Control Room like carelessly flung dice. Many of the men sat on the floor, hugging their knees; only Eddie Green wore an American uniform—the rest looked like bedraggled German sailors.

"Okay," Tyler said, stepping forward, "listen up. As senior man, I'm in charge. Understood? Okay. We're heading to England. Land's End."

Confused expressions blossomed on faces around him; Tyler was unsure whether this was in response to his assertion of command, or his announcement of their new course.

Tyler continued: "There are nine of us, plus our prisoner. That's enough to put together a barebones watch. Eddie, you have a chance to check for provisions? How are we fixed for chow?"

Green glanced around, obviously not relishing delivering bad news.

The Chief said, "Eddie, we all know this boat was waitin' for resupply. You think anybody's gonna blame you?"

"Well," Green said, "we do got some potatoes, some canned cabbage. . . . We'll make do, sir."

Suddenly, from aft, Tank ducked through the hatchway, grease-smudged, carrying a wrench; all eyes—and flashlights—turned to the machinist mate.

"Guess you guys figured out by now the batteries are deader than a dead dog's dick. Whatever juice we had left got sucked dry when we maneuvered."

"What about the diesels?" Tyler asked.

Tank jerked a thumb backward, like a hitchhiker in a bad mood. "Starboard side's a goddamn wreck. Anybody's got a dry dock in his back pocket, now's the time."

"You bearin' anything but bad tidings?" the Chief asked.

Tank shrugged. "Port side's got potential. Whoever the Krauts had wrenchin' on that thing don't know a piston head from his girlfriend's left titty."

Tyler asked, "Can you fix it?"

Tank grinned, oil smeared on his teeth. "I know titties and I know engines. Anybody can make this ol' girl purr, it's me."

"Good. Good! Get on it, Tank."

Nodding, smiling tightly, Tank ducked back aft.

Tyler turned to Rabbit. "How many fish we got left?"

"Just one, sir," the torpedoman said. "In the stern line. Which is, by the way, busted to shit."

"What's wrong with it?"

"High pressure line's bleeding air from somewhere."

Like a schoolkid, young Trigger raised his hand. "Sir?"

"What, Trigger?"

"Why can't we just radio for help? Fire off a Mayday and just sit tight till we get rescued?"

"Mr. Hirsch," Tyler said, "would you care to explain?"

Stepping forward, the balding, professorial Hirsch said, "Using the radio is impossible. If we transmit, the Germans will direction-find our signal to a grid where they just happen to be missing a pair of U-boats. And if they even suspect we have the Enigma machine, they'll change their entire coding system, immediately, and everything we've accomplished, every man who died, our entire mission, would be for nothing."

Silence draped the Control Room, then Mazzola spoke up. "The mission's over. It went to hell. The Skipper's dead, we're stranded. There ain't no mission."

"Mazzola—" Tyler began.

But Hirsch raised a hand. "Gentlemen, let me be very clear: despite what's happened, we still must deliver the Enigma into Allied hands. And we must do so without the Germans ever knowing we have it. This mission has just begun."

Though this had been a thorough explanation, and by his way of thinking a convincing one, Tyler knew his boys weren't entirely buying it: the slight, bookish Hirsch just couldn't sell it properly. Tyler was wondering if he should amplify what Hirsch had said, when Wentz spoke up.

"Mr. Tyler," the radioman said, "if we head for England, it's gonna take us right smack through the Western Approaches."

"That's right," Tyler said.

Mazzola, eyes popping, said, "That's Jerry's backyard, crawlin' with U-boats! That's fuckin' Wolf Pack Central!"

"And we got nothin' to defend ourselves with," Rabbit said, " 'cept one broken-ass torpedo!"

"I say we use the radio," Mazzola said.

The Chief, glowering, spat, "Who asked you?"

"Use it," Mazzola continued, "and take our god-damn chances."

"Yeah!" Rabbit chimed.

Tightly, Klough said, "Can it, you two—"

"It's what the Skipper woulda done," Mazzola insisted.

"Get it through your thick heads," Klough said, almost yelling, "the Skipper's dead. Got it? Dead. So shut the hell up."

Mazzola shut up.

The Chief's defense only served to undercut Tyler's confidence more; all around him, the men were challenging his judgment. He could feel his grip on authority slipping. . . .

"You think I don't wish we had the Skipper here," Tyler blurted, "to get his read on this? Well, we don't. You think I have all the answers? Well, I don't. You think I know what to do? Well . . ."

Shaking his head, tired, overwhelmed by everything cast upon him, Tyler moved quickly through the forward hatch, leaving behind a stunned crew who had not exactly received the kind of rallying speech they had wanted to hear.

And when they looked to the Chief for support or an explanation, all they saw was a stony expression and cold, disgusted eyes.

Whether that disgust was in response to them, or their departed "Skipper," no one could tell.

Finally Mazzola spoke up. "Nothin' wrong with us that havin' a goddamn *captain* aboard wouldn't cure."

Not knowing that they did, in fact, have a captain aboard—the real captain of the U-571, currently in custody.

CHAINED TO A stanchion in the canary-yellow
cubbyhole of the galley, leaning against the oven,
Kapitanlieutnant Gunthar Wassner watched
through the nearby hatchway, which provided a
frame for a portrait of a man at work: the sailor
called Tank repairing the diesels of the U-571. The
deft, skillful overhauling the muscular sailor carried out made the former captain of the U-boat
wish this dexterous hulking beast had been one of
his own crew.

Wassner watched with a strange sense of pride,
as the sailor's hands on the throttle gradually raised
the rpm until the rows of rocker arms fell and rose,
fell and rose, in an ever faster motion that became
a familiar blur.

His ship was running. Soon, Wassner knew, the
batteries of the U-571 would be recharged, and the
boat would be fully alive again—his dream of a
few hours ago had become a reality.

But the sub was in the hands of the enemy now,
and—even as he watched the blur of the pistons
with a proprietary gaze—Wassner knew that his

157

duty, his mission, was to find a way to disable his ship, to stop the Americans, to keep them from taking the secrets of the Enigma decoder and of the U-boat itself to the Allied command.

To scuttle the U-571.

A few hours later, under a perfect sunny blue sky that made the storm of the night before seem a bizarre bad dream, the U-571—its batteries recharged, its engines purring—was but a small dot in a vast ocean, cruising slowly east, toward Europe.

From the bridge the current captain of the boat—Lieutenant Andrew J. Tyler—watched with satisfaction as his ship sliced through the swells, spray washing over the deck. The brawny mechanical genius who had made this possible—Machinist Mate Clemens, Tank—was crossing to stern. He watched Tank inspect a fueling connection, then—heartened that all was well—Tyler moved down the ladder into the empty conning tower, its helm unmanned, Trigger having been assigned to the alternate helm in the Control Room.

Tyler was about to descend the rest of the way, when he heard voices below—and the words froze him.

"Hell," Mazzola was saying. "This whole damn dodge is screwy. What are we doin', risking our skins for a goddamn typewriter?"

The men were down there performing a task Tyler had assigned—tying English-translation tags onto valves—while the Chief was trying to make heads or tails out of a schematic they'd located of the trim and drain system.

"It's not a typewriter," Wentz said, but he didn't sound convinced, himself.

"Fuck if it ain't!" Mazzola said. "It's got keys like a typewriter, it's got a case like a typewriter, it's a friggin' *typewriter*—and I say this is screwy, gettin' our asses killed over the hunk of junk."

"Navy says it's important," the Chief said matter-of-factly, "it's important."

"Important," Mazzola snorted.

"More important than you," the Chief said, firmly now, "more important than me, or any of you."

"That's your opinion, Chief."

"That's the Navy's opinion—so it *is* my opinion, and, guess what, Mazzola—it's *yours*, too. Got that?"

Mazzola said nothing.

The Chief continued. "So the Navy has us deliverin' a typewriter. Well, I say we're gonna drop that hunk of junk right in the brasshats' laps, or die tryin'. That ain't screwy, sailor—that's our job. Our duty."

Up on the ladder in the conning tower, Tyler found himself smiling, reassured by the Chief's speech, Klough's forceful handling of this minor insurrection.

Then Mazzola posed another question, down there, that wiped away Tyler's smile.

"How come *you* ain't in charge, Chief? You got the years. Scuttlebutt was, Dahlgren was gettin' Tyler's ass kicked out of the Navy."

The Chief blew up. "Stow that shit, sailor! Right now! You served with Lieutenant Tyler, you know that's a buncha backstabbin' bilge. He was a fine XO, and Dahlgren respected him for it."

"An XO ain't a CO."

"Well, he's your CO now, and you will respect the man as such. You don't talk this shit, you don't *think* this shit. Am I understood? All of you?"

Silence, below. Tyler felt sick, clinging to the ladder.

Then a few chastened voices muttered, "Yes, sir."

And Tyler scrambled back up onto the bridge, to get some air, and try not to puke.

Kapitanlieutnant Wassner—chained to the ladder at the left of the galley—had been entrusted with a can opener. His rather demeaning position was to assist the black cook, whose name was Eddie; but this menial function was fine with Wassner—it reflected how fully the Americans had bought the lie he'd fed them: that he had been a lowly electrician aboard the U-571.

As the black cook stirred a pot of soup, Wassner opened cans of cabbage, sneaking looks through the open hatchway into the petty officers' quarters, where the intellectual-looking American called Hirsch sat on a nearby bunk, studying the boat's crew manifest.

In the very respectable, unaccented German that had aided in the raiders' masquerade, Hirsch asked him, "Tell me, Electrician's Mate Bohler, how long have you been aboard the U-571?"

Wassner looked up from his can-opening, saying in German, "Only four months, sir. Stupid of me to volunteer, really."

"And why is that?"

"On the *Tirpitz*," Wassner said, doing his best to seem a guileless, grateful survivor, "I had my own bunk and all the fresh air the sea had to offer."

Hirsch's finger had stopped, as he traced names on the manifest. Wassner repressed a smile, knowing the American had no doubt landed on the name of the real Bohler, who had indeed transferred from the *Tirpitz*.

The black cook held up a palm. "That's enough for now, Schicklgruber. You follow me?"

Wassner winced, as if comprehending this simple English was difficult for him. "No more . . . open . . . can?"

"Yeah, yeah, no more open can. Hey, Mr. Hirsch—you think I can trust this Heinie with a potato peeler?"

Hirsch smiled thinly. "I believe so, Eddie."

As this exchange passed, Wassner had managed to drop the can opener into his boot.

Soon the true captain of the U-571 had been equipped with a tiny potato peeler and was flaying slivers of skin from what the cook referred to as spuds. About this time, the short, seasoned sailor they called the Chief came strutting into the tiny galley, helping himself to a cup of coffee.

"I see ya got yourself a mother's little helper, Eddie," the Chief said, pouring himself a second cup.

"Sure do, Chief." A white smile blossomed in

the black face. "It's that master race we been hearin' so much about, gettin' a taste of good ol' American KP."

"We'll make a sailor out of this sad sack, yet."

"You bet, Chief. He's gonna scrub the deck for us, next."

"Make sure it shines, Eddie." The Chief gave Wassner a smirk and sauntered out with the two tin cups of steaming coffee.

And Wassner, peeling potatoes like an enlisted man, used his right bootheel to further tug down his left pant leg over the boot with the appropriated can opener in it.

In the captain's cabin—which was little more than a narrow recess separated from the main passageway by a green curtain he'd drawn back—Tyler discovered a well-used gray leather jacket on a hook. He removed the jacket, tried it on—it seemed just a little big, but this was the captain's jacket, and he was the captain now, and he left the damn thing on.

He stretched out on the padded bench, which could be turned into the captain's bunk, noting silhouettes of ships carved into the oak paneling next to him—the ships the U-571 had sunk. Also arrayed were snapshots and official photos of Kriegsmarine pomp and circumstance, including the German crew of this boat standing in formation on their submarine, and another of a clean-shaven U-boat commander receiving a medal from Hitler himself.

Chief Klough entered with two tin cups of hot

coffee. "Try this swill, sir—you'll learn why those bastards are so damn mean."

Tyler, still stretched out, nodded toward the tiny table where the former captain of the U-571 had no doubt kept his war log up to date. "Leave it, would you?"

Klough set the cup down.

Tyler expected the Chief to go on about his business, but the man was staring down at him, looming over him, steaming coffee cup in hand.

"Something on your mind, Chief?"

"We got a long way to go, Lieutenant. You ready for what's ahead?"

"Do I have a choice?"

The Chief said nothing, just flinched a non-smile and sipped his coffee.

Tyler turned to the photos plastered to the paneling. "Look at these sons of bitches. Spit and polish to the gills."

Chief leaned in. "Yes, sir. They're a pretty bunch of Nazis."

"Did you know my pop was a fisherman?"

Klough leaned back out. "No, sir."

"Well, he was. Had a sixty-footer he ran all over the Gulf. Summers, I used to run the deck, all day, all night, seven days a week."

"Got your first taste for the sea."

"Yeah, and also smell. That tub was rotten to the gunnels, reekin' with the stink of fish, and a noisy two-stroke diesel that didn't smell much better. See, Chief, I love my pop, but I swore I'd never skipper a bucket like that, no way in hell. I saw myself standing on the bridge of a battleship, dress whites, four gold stripes, crew manning the rail in their crackerjacks. A real captain."

The Chief's expression was unreadable. He took another sip, a thoughtful one. Then he said, "Mr. Tyler, permission to speak freely."

"Of course, Chief."

"If you wanted a fancy uniform and a big shiny boat to impress your daddy, you shoulda got a job steering the Staten Island ferry."

Frowning, Tyler sat up.

Klough pressed on. "You wonder why these men aren't loyal to you—I mean, you were a popular XO, used to hoist the suds with these gobs. But that's over. You got to stop thinking of yourself as a two-striper, even though that's exactly what I see, a two-striper in way over his head."

"I know I'm the captain, Chief. I know it all too well."

"You're the captain, all right, but you don't know it near well enough. In this man's navy, a commanding officer is a mighty and terrible thing, a man to be feared, a man to be respected. A captain don't hold a goddamn discussion group, like you did last night, back there in Control. A captain is all knowing, all powerful, and he don't never say he don't have the answers, that he don't know what to do. Those are words that'll torpedo a crew faster and deader than anything the fuckin' Krauts got."

"Chief . . ."

"You're the skipper now. Dahlgren's gone, God rest his soul, and you're the skipper and the skipper always knows what to do whether he does or not."

Tyler didn't know what to say; he just stared

back at the Chief, in a frank unstated admission that he knew what Klough had said was true, and right.

And Chief stared at him, or anyway past him. . . .

Suddenly Klough leaned in, and over, the reclining Tyler, to get a closer look at the photos tacked to the oak paneling.

"Shit," Klough said quietly.

And then the Chief covered the lower portion of the face of the commander in the photo—the captain receiving Adolf's congratulations—which left the upper half of that face exposed, in much the same way a full beard might.

"Shit!" Klough said. "That's . . ."

"Our prisoner!" Tyler said, flying off the bench.

But the Chief was already racing down the passageway, aft. Tyler caught up just as they rushed past Hirsch, seated on a bunk near the open hatchway to the tiny galley, where their prisoner—a potato peeler in hand, sitting on a ladder step—was eyeing Eddie Green, bent over to search a locker for cookware, like the cook was another potato to skin.

"Eddie, on your feet!" the Chief said, out of breath, coming to a stop at the doorway. Tyler almost piled into him. "That SOB is the captain!"

Eddie rose, backed away, though in that cubicle the two men were still close. "No kiddin'. From the half-ass way he peels potatoes, I had him pegged for latrine orderly."

"Search him, Eddie," the Chief said.

The mess steward nodded and snatched the

peeler away from the man, then hauled him to his feet and began to pat him down.

Coming up from behind, Hirsch edged between the Chief and Tyler.

"This is Captain Wassner," Hirsch said. "I read his name in the crew manifest."

Green was slipping a hand into the German captain's left boot; he came back with a pilfered can opener. "Well, ain't we the shifty little shitheel—who were you plannin' to open with this?"

Wassner glowered, then Hirsch said, in German, "Welcome to our ship, Captain Wassner. We have much to talk about."

And Wassner glowered some more.

Tyler said, "Chief, lay aft with the prisoner and chain him to a bulkhead, where Tank can keep an eye on him. This bastard'll know a hundred ways to scuttle his own boat."

The Chief nodded, clearly pleased by the authority of Tyler's words.

Tyler went on: "Now no one touches this SOB, understand? He's a valuable prisoner of war."

Almost beaming, Hirsch said, "You're absolutely correct, Lieutenant. He's as valuable as this captured U-boat itself."

The Chief began uncuffing Wassner, who turned to Tyler and said, in easy, perfectly nuanced and nearly accentless English, "Lieutenant, why don't you tell these men the truth?"

Hearing such flawless English emanating from this prisoner who had previously spoken only a basic, broken version shocked Tyler, and everyone else.

"You have no chance," Wassner was saying. "The Kriegsmarine will never stand for this. When it is realized that you have the Enigma, every ship in our navy will be sent to destroy you."

Tyler said nothing; cold rage crawled through him—and cold fear.

Wassner was still talking, turning to the others, now. "But of course I could be wrong. After all, this ship is in such perfect condition, and you are led by so experienced and strong a captain. How could you lose?"

"Can it," the Chief said, shoving Wassner, unchained now, toward the aft hatchway. "And move it."

Over his shoulder, Wassner said, "This boy is taking you to your graves. You are dead men, unless you surrender to our mercy. It's only a question of time."

From the tube came Rabbit's strident voice: "Aircraft off the port bow quarter, two thousand yards!"

As alarmed expressions blossomed around him, Tyler found himself looking into the grinning visage of the other captain of the U-571, who was saying, "You see how I speak the truth? It's over for you, already."

"Plug that leak, Chief," Tyler said, tossing a dishrag to the Chief, and rushing out.

Behind him, he could hear the Chief saying, "Aye, aye, sir," as Klough stuffed the dirty rag into Wassner's mouth.

Then the Chief tossed Wassner to the mess steward, said, "Chain the bastard up, Eddie," and hustled forward, tagging after his captain.

13

SILHOUETTED LIKE A birthmark on the face of the sun, the plane—not even discernible as a plane, without binoculars—was the only blemish on this perfect sunny day, the sky ocean-blue, the ocean sky-blue, the breeze stirring waves so gently you would have thought a bored God had dipped a toe in.

"Too late to dive, damnit," Tyler said, looking through the binoculars. "He's seen us. . . ."

On the U-571's bridge, Tyler—wearing Wassner's gray leather jacket—had just climbed up to join Rabbit, Mazzola and Trigger, who'd been standing watch.

"I'm sorry, sir," Rabbit said, with the curdled expression of a kid admitting to a parent he'd messed up. "He dropped right out of the sun, on top of us!"

"Why the hell *can't* we dive, sir?" Mazzola asked.

"If we do," Tyler said, lowering the binocs for a moment, "that pilot'll know something's up."

Mazzola, wincing in confused irritation, gestured

with upraised palms. "But how do we know whether it's one of ours or one of theirs?"

"We better *hope* it's one of theirs."

"What?"

Flashing a tiny wry smile to the Brooklynite, Tyler said, "You might want to reflect on how a US plane might react to that big swastika on the side of this ship."

Mazzola looked down wide-eyed at himself in the Kriegsmarine fatigues. "Shit. We're fuckin' Nazis!"

"Let's hope we can pass for it, anyway. . . . Rabbit, Trigger, sidle over by the flak gun—not like you're anticipating any trouble, but close enough to respond to an order."

"Aye, sir," Rabbit said, Trigger echoing that, as they crossed to the anti-aircraft gun, aft.

Tyler peered up at the blue sky, wincing at the sunlight that was still in back of the aircraft, which was finally acquiring some definition, as it dropped beneath the sun's fiery ball. He could make out wings, fuselage. . . .

"German," Tyler said. "That could be a break."

"Some break," Mazzola said.

"Looks like it's doing long-range recon." Tyler frowned in thought. "What the hell's it doing way out here?"

He handed the binocs to Mazzola, and turned to Rabbit and Trigger, standing near the flak gun, casually to the distant eye, poised for action to Tyler's.

"Here's what we're gonna do, boys," Tyler said, almost lightly. "We're gonna let this Heinie flyboy think we're all buddies in the Reich. When he flies by, we're gonna smile, we're gonna wave."

Mazzola scowled. "Are you kidding . . . sir?"

"We're just another U-boat, returning from a successful patrol."

"Come on, sir—we're sittin' ducks! We can shoot first, and blow that bastard outa the sky. You know we can!"

"Have you ever shot down a plane before, Mazzola? Rabbit? Trigger?"

"Gotta start somewhere, Lieutenant," Mazzola said. "Let's blast the bum before he blasts us."

The Chief's words about discussion groups flashed through Tyler's mind; how could he stop this questioning of his every command? What the hell was wrong with them? What the hell was wrong with him?

The plane was descending, coming in for a look.

"Mazzola, we shoot and miss, and he's gonna radio it in. And then that plane will be the least of our problems."

"Aw, Jesus," Mazzola said. "Here he comes. . . ."

The German aircraft had dropped to an altitude of fifty feet—and it was right in front of them, larger every second, coming right the hell at them, the whine of its engines growing to a growl, its shadow gliding blackly over the blue waters.

Tyler glanced at Rabbit, whose hands gripped the handles of the flak gun, the boy's face splashed with anxiety as he nervously shot a look at Trigger standing next to him.

"Easy, Rabbit. Trigger, take it easy now. To this

character, we're just an ordinary U-boat, four good little Nazis on the bridge. . . ."

But Tyler could understand Rabbit's uneasiness, because he felt it himself, wondering if he was doing the right thing, pushing the apprehension down as the plane got bigger in their vision, the growl building to a roar.

"I can see him," Rabbit said, jaw clenched, sweat trickling down his face in glistening streams. "I can see the pilot!"

"Far as he knows," Tyler said, smiling up at the plane, "we're all playing on the same team. Everybody wave."

And the four Americans in German uniforms on the bridge of the U-boat waved hello, eagerly, at the oncoming plane, approaching at one hundred twenty miles per hour.

He's got us right in his gunsights, Tyler thought, and grinned, and waved, heart hammering, staring right into the four snouts of the front-mounted machine guns. *If he's going to shoot, now's the time . . . now's the time.*

The aircraft thundered over them, whooshing across the length of the boat, lashing their clothing and their flesh with its mechanically whipped wind, so close that when they looked up at its metal belly, they could have counted the goddamn rivets; then they turned and waved good-bye, their grins for real now as the plane headed away, hope leaping inside Tyler.

He had done the right thing.

But as the plane climbed, it began a tight, banking turn, coming back, to begin circling overhead.

As they all squinted up at the plane, hovering in the sunshine, Mazzola said, "Jesus, what he's up to now?"

"Oh shit," Rabbit said, dancing at the flak gun like a child in need of a bathroom, "oh shit, shit, shit . . ."

"Steady, Rabbit," Tyler said. "Everybody— steady. All our pal wants is a little closer look."

"At what?" The blood had drained from Mazzola's face. "He musta spotted somethin'—somethin' musta looked hinky to him. . . ."

"He's just playing it cautious." Tyler kept waving. "Everybody stay cool."

"He saw something," Mazzola insisted. "Why the hell else would he be hangin' around?"

And the plane kept circling, like a vulture waiting for them to die . . . or to swoop in and help them die.

"Son of a bitch," Rabbit said, staring up at the plane. "He's gonna attack us!"

Tyler could see in Rabbit's expression the boy's confidence in his commander's strategy dissolving.

"All due respect, sir," Mazzola said, waving halfheartedly, "I think we oughta take the bastard out."

"Keeping waving, sailor."

"This is crazy!" Mazzola yelled, jaw muscles jumping, grinding his teeth, apparently barely able to contain himself. "You're gonna get us fuckin' killed!"

Now the plane descended into a wide, banking turn, engine howling like a vengeful banshee. Every sailor in the ship would hear that, Tyler

knew; the fear on this bridge would have spread by now within the boat below—lives at stake, lives he had risked by following his instinct, his training.

Rabbit was muttering to himself, either swearing or praying, maybe both, and—as the pressure mounted—Tyler knew the boy was starting to crack. Poor Trigger was glancing between the nervous Rabbit and the apparently cool Tyler, wondering who to follow.

"Keep waving," Tyler said, as the plane turned to overfly the sub from the stern.

"No more," Mazzola said, stopping, "no more waving at a goddamn German plane."

"Keep waving, sailor. I'm warning you."

"Goddamnit, he's comin' in for the kill! He's gonna strafe us!" Mazzola yelled at Rabbit: "Shoot him! *Fucking shoot him!*"

Rabbit unlatched the flak gun mount and took aim; with the plane coming right at him, it was a subtle shift that the pilot might not be able to read, but Tyler knew the danger the act created for them.

"Belay that, Rabbit!" Tyler could feel his face reddening with rage. "Do not fire that weapon, I repeat, *do not fire that weapon!*"

At the flak gun, Rabbit was a headlight-frozen deer, the plane bearing down on him, its engine screaming.

Tyler screamed, too: "Acknowledge me, sailor! *Rabbit!*"

Mazzola had completely lost it. "We're gonna fuckin' die! Blast the bastard! *Blast* him, Rabbit!"

"Seaman Parker," Tyler said, watching that plane grow larger and larger, its engines shrieking louder and louder, "I am *ordering* you to hold your fire! Get your hands off that weapon—*now*!"

Instead, Rabbit jerked the trigger!

And produced an impotent *klik*.

Relief flooded through Tyler at the flak gun's failure to fire, as the German plane buzzed over them—not strafing them, just moving on, climbing, banking away toward the horizon, tipping its wings in good-bye—the pilot's way of waving back at them.

Tyler looked at Rabbit, who had cleared the weapon and was examining the antiaircraft shell, holding it in his hands like a baby.

"Primer's dented," Rabbit said timidly.

"Fuckin' dud," Mazzola said.

"Mazzola," Tyler said.

Mazzola turned, saying, "Yes, sir," or trying to, because only part of it got out before Tyler slammed his fist into the sailor's face, a good hard right hand.

Reeling backward, almost going down, getting stopped by the bridge railing, Mazzola raised a hand to his bloody nose.

"Any questions about that?" Tyler asked tightly.

Swallowing, Mazzola clutched his gushing nose, leaning against the railing.

Getting right in the cowering sailor's face, Tyler said, "Next time I'll shoot you, since there's no time for a court-martial out here." He whirled to address the stunned audience of Rabbit and Trigger, as well as Mazzola. "Where did you sorry sons of bitches get the idea this was a goddamn democracy? *I* am the *captain* of this boat—is there any part of that sentence that you don't understand?"

Rabbit lowered his gaze. Trigger swallowed. Mazzola tried to breathe through the bloody nose.

"My orders are exactly that: *orders.*" Tyler jerked a thumb at his chest. "There will be no more discussions about whether or not my orders are worth carrying out. You will carry out my orders, without hesitation, without question. Otherwise, I will shoot your sorry asses and toss you overboard with the rest of the dead fucking Nazis. Anyone care to discuss that?"

The three sailors, averting their eyes from Tyler's hard gaze, nodded, Rabbit muttering, "No, sir."

"Sir!" Trigger said. He thrust a finger out toward the sea. "Mast on the horizon, sir!"

Tyler raised his binoculars and aimed them toward where the boy was pointing. It was more than just a mast: the superstructure of a warship could be made out against the sky, as could the blinking of a signal light emanating from its deck.

"Hell," Tyler said. "That's a Nazi destroyer. That plane was running a recon screen for it."

Tyler lowered his binoculars, and caught Mazzola and Rabbit trading looks that mingled worry and relief, reflecting the comment Trigger made: "Thank God we didn't shoot it down!"

"We have to answer that signal," Tyler said, and shouted down the hatch: "Mr. Hirsch! Lay to the bridge!" Below, the Chief echoed his order, as Tyler turned to Trigger, saying, "Get the signal lamp."

"Aye, aye, sir," Trigger said, and scooted down the ladder through the conning tower.

Tyler yelled down the hatch again: "Chief, stand by to dive."

Below the Chief echoed: "Rig for dive!"

Then Hirsch was scrambling up onto the bridge, Tyler handing him the binocs.

"That German warship out there's talking to us," Tyler said. "See what's on its mind."

Hirsch gazed through the binocs, squinting, reading, translating. "Baker . . . Affirm . . . Dog . . . Sugar . . . Yoke . . . Prep . . . Baker . . . Affirm." He lowered the glasses and said, "Okay, it's repeating." He raised them again. " 'Stop engines,' they say. 'Report status.' "

Tyler chewed on that for a moment, then asked, "Think they're onto us, Mr. Hirsch?"

Hirsch lowered the glasses again and looked blankly at Tyler. "Frankly, I don't know. What I mean is, I can't tell." Then the bookish officer's eyes tightened, and he reached out and gripped Tyler's arm. "But for God's sake, man, don't dive— if we raise *any* suspicions, they'll know we're not Germans."

Trigger came up from below, signal lamp in hand.

Mulling it over, Tyler said, "Damn. If they come alongside us, they'll figure us out in a few minutes . . . if it takes 'em that long."

Hirsch's gaze behind the wireframes was firm. "You have to answer their signal, Lieutenant."

Tyler sighed, then, thinking aloud, said, "All right. Suppose our boat, the U-571, was shelled by a British destroyer during the rendezvous, and the resupply boat was sunk."

"That's good." Hirsch was nodding. "That's good."

"You could tell 'em we've only got one engine running and are limping back to port."

"Good." Hirsch's eyes flashed with thought. "And how about I add that our radio's broken?"

"Yes. Yes, that's a nice addition to our sad story. Think we need anything else, Mr. Hirsch?"

Hirsch shook his head, said, "That should do nicely," and took the signal lamp from Trigger; soon the lamp's *klik, klik, klik* was replying to the enemy warship.

Then Hirsch, finished with his task, looked to Tyler and raised his eyebrows with a shrug.

Gnawing his lip, Tyler muttered, "Let's hope they buy it. Sweet Jesus, let them buy it. . . ."

"Stand by," Hirsch said, eyes on the ship now. "Reply coming."

Even without the binoculars, the destroyer was visible now—a tiny, ominous speck on the horizon. It winked at them, and winked and winked, responding to Hirsch's message.

Finally, Hirsch—binocs up—said, " 'Acknowledge. Steer new course. One four zero.' " Hirsch, alarmed, turned to Tyler. "Damn! They want to escort us south."

"Oh hell no," Tyler said. "We won't be doing that. You tell them we are only making eight knots and to proceed without us."

Hirsch nodded, and returned to his signaling, sending more *klik*s out across the water. The reply was immediate.

" 'We salute your bravery,' they say," Hirsch

read through the binoculars. " 'We will not leave you . . . to face predators. . . . Change course as directed.' "

Tyler slapped the railing. "God *damn!*"

"Lieutenant," Hirsch said, rather gently, "we can't go with them."

"Of course we can't."

"And we can't dive, either."

"Damned if we do, damned if we don't."

"Exactly. Can you think of another option, Lieutenant? Because I sure as hell can't."

"So we can't go with them," Tyler said softly, starting to smile, "and we can't dive . . . but there is something we *can* do."

Confused looks blossomed on the bridge; but Tyler was grinning.

"Mr. Hirsch, I'm going below to initiate my plan," Tyler said. "Wait three minutes and send a distress signal. Tell our good friends over there that we have an engine fire—and we're going down."

"I don't understand," Hirsch said.

"The U-571 is about to sink," Tyler said, and went below.

14

IN THE FORWARD torpedo room of the U-571, Rabbit and Trigger were loading up a tube—not with a torpedo, but clothing, blankets, mattresses, bottles, papers, empty cans, plates, cups, broken radio gear, virtually anything and everything that was not nailed down and could be spared. Nearby Mazzola was kicking the shit out of a wooden locker, turning it into rubble, then gathering up the splintered boards and chunks of wood and shoving them in the tube where they could join the other trash and treasure.

In the rear torpedo room, Kapitanlieutnant Gunthar Wassner had not yet figured out what these damn Americans were up to. Faking that your ship had been hit and was sinking, during a depth-charge barrage, was a commonplace tactic. But no depth charges were dropping—what in hell was this for?

Seated on a nearby bunk, handcuffed to its metal sideboard, Wassner watched, confused, curious, as the brawny sailor called Tank, in a T-shirt, muscles rippling and basted with sweat and grease, poured fuel oil into a bucket crammed with shredded clothing.

Leaning his face near his hands, the former captain of the U-571 finally managed, with captive fingers, to pull that dirty rag from his mouth. Ungagged, he spit several times, trying to clear his palate of the greasy taste.

As Wassner did this, the brute was lifting the bucket with its oil-soaked cloth, carrying it like a boy returning with fresh water from a well, and hanging it on a hook under the after torpedo loading hatch.

"What are you doing?" Wassner asked him.

The brute turned and smirked at the German officer. "Adolf speaks! You know what a barbecue is?"

"No."

"Well, stick around—you're guest of honor at this one." The brute opened a locker, reached inside and grabbed a potash respirator, tossing the mask onto the bunk next to Wassner.

"Might wanna put that on," the sailor advised.

The voice of Tyler, the American "captain," came over the intercom speaker: "Okay, Tank— pop the hatch and light 'er up!"

The brute slipped on his own mask, then produced a box of kitchen matches from his fatigues and lit one, holding the flame high for Wassner to see. Then he dropped the match into the bucket, creating an immediate *whoosh* of flame, and—almost as immediate—thick, black, roiling smoke.

Despite his cuffed hands, Wassner managed to get the mask on, while the brute—chuckling at the

German's difficulty—yanked open the torpedo loading hatch between the big E-motors.

As black smoke billowed from the bucket, the brute tipped it forward so that as much as possible would stream up into the torpedo tube. Taking this in, Wassner was not sure what the would-be captain of his ship was up to, with this feigned sinking . . .

. . . but he knew he must do his best to thwart that effort.

Captain Wassner owed it to his dead boys, to his captured ship, and, most of all, to himself.

On the bridge of the U-571—under a beautiful blue sky suddenly smudged by the streaming black smoke from the after hatch of the sub—Lieutenant Andrew Tyler, binoculars up, watched the destroyer as Hirsch used the signal light, *klik, klik, klik*ing a repeated distress signal.

The warship was closer now, much more than a dot on the horizon—more like a child's toy in a big tub, a scale model replica of intricate detail. As smoke trailed into the sky behind him, Tyler prayed the children playing with that "toy" destroyer would be fooled by his schoolyard prank.

When Hirsch lowered the signal lamp, Tyler handed him the binocs, so the German-speaking Naval Reserve lieutenant could read the destroyer's response. Oh how Tyler hoped there would be a response!

Finally, light winked at them from the deck of the toy boat.

"They acknowledge our distress signal," Hirsch

said, beaming, relieved. "Looks like they're buying it."

Tyler leaned into the voice tube. "Tank, put out that fire pronto, and secure the hatch! Chief, flood those tanks. Make it look real! Make it look good!"

Below, he knew, his orders would be swiftly carried out, the Chief spinning handwheels, Trigger working the planes. And even as smoke continued to spill into the sky from the after hatch, Tank's reassuring words came from the voice tube: "Control, fire is out!"

Tyler and Hirsch traded quick, hopeful glances.

This could work, Tyler thought, *this could really work.*

Wassner had watched and waited.

In the rear torpedo room, a compartment clouded with nasty thick smoke, Wassner—protected by the mask the sailor had so thoughtfully provided him— had watched as the brute used a bulky cylindrical fire extinguisher to spray the smoldering clothing in the bucket, putting the fire out quickly.

Then the muscular sailor had set down the extinguisher and grasped the hatch handle and swung it shut with a satisfying clank. Crossing to the voice tube, removing his potash mask as he went, the brute sent word forward to his commander that the fire was indeed out.

The brute had not seen Wassner slipping his handcuffs around and through the space where the metal sideboard didn't quite meet the wall, allowing it to fold up; nor had he seen Wassner—still handcuffed—get to his feet and move toward him.

And when the strapping sailor turned from the voice tube, the German captain was waiting, to punch him in the crotch, a two-handed handcuffed blow that doubled this Tank instantly over—and all the muscles in America couldn't have helped him.

Then Wassner scooped the heavy fire extinguisher from the deck and swung the steel tube up, catching the doubled-over sailor smack in the forehead with its bottom, knocking him back, and out, dropping him rudely on the deck in a big unconscious pile.

Smiling tightly, the still-cuffed Wassner lifted the Luger from the holster on the out-cold brute's belt, shoved it in his own waistband, then frisked the boy's fatigues, quickly finding the handcuff keys.

Soon Wassner's cuffs were on the brute's wrists instead, the German captain fixing his prisoner to a properly sturdy pipe near enough so that he hadn't had to lug the hefty sailor far.

With a satisfying sigh—glad to be in charge of his ship again—Wassner stopped the diesels, engaged the reverse cam and restarted it. The sound of the boat vibrating, as the screwshaft turned in reverse, was music to his ears—every bit as sweet as the Bing Crosby and Billie Holiday records he had brought aboard with him.

As the boat was rigged for dive, Tyler and Hirsch left the bridge, climbing down the ladder through the conning tower, Hirsch first, and just as Tyler was dogging the hatch, the ship began to shake, to shudder, as if the U-571 itself were afraid.

Sliding down the ladder into the Control Room, Tyler moved to the Chief's post, where Klough was shaking his head, pointing to several valve and gauge indicators that still glowed red.

"Why don't we have a greenboard?" Tyler demanded.

"Engine room isn't ready," the Chief said, gesturing to specific red lights on the board, "and we've lost hydraulics. Plus, the ballast tank vents don't wanna open."

Grabbing the intercom mike, Tyler testily said, "Tank, quit holding us up—secure the diesel and ready the engine room to dive! Acknowledge."

Tyler waited, exchanging troubled glances with Klough. Then into the mike, he spat, "Tank! Report!"

Nothing.

"Mazzola," Tyler said, "haul ass back there and see what the hell's going on."

Mazzola said, "Aye, sir," and ducked through the hatch and hustled down the passageway. Tyler watched as Mazzola sprinted through the crew quarters and even caught a glimpse of him rushing by Eddie in the galley.

Striding over to the board, where red lights still stubbornly glowed, Tyler said, "We've got to take this baby down."

"We do it now," the Chief said, "we'll go down, all right—we just won't come back up."

Seconds passed like minutes, and Tyler said, "What the fuck is going on back there?"

That was when they heard the gunshots.

*   *   *

Wassner had been on his way to dog that hatchway when he spotted the dark, curly-haired sailor rushing down the passageway toward him. The German ducked back deeper within the torpedo room, stepping to one side, as the sailor—Wassner had heard him called Mazzola, a damned Italian who should be fighting on the Axis side—charged into the still-smoky rear torpedo room. As the sailor stopped short, spotting his unconscious fellow crew member—the handcuffed-to-a-pipe Tank—Wassner materialized out of the fog of drifting black fumes and leveled the gun at him.

The German might have spared the Italian, not out of mercy—Wassner would have no mercy for these savage raiders who had butchered the boys of his ship—but to preserve his limited Luger ammunition.

If the boy had fled, that is: instead the Italian chose not to withdraw, rather rushing headlong at Wassner, with only a scowl and a war cry to offer up against his Luger.

Wassner shot twice, the report echoing in the iron chamber like brittle thunder, and the Italian called Mazzola took both rounds in the chest.

Yet still he came!

The wounded sailor threw himself at Wassner, tackling the German, taking him down, stunning him physically and mentally, and suddenly the strong young bleeding sailor was trying to wrest the Luger from Wassner's hands, as they wrestled on the cold deck.

Wassner could feel his wrist giving way, as the Italian—grinning at him like a skull, the sweaty smell of the boy in the German's nostrils—forced the gun back on him, and the hand over his hand forced Wassner to squeeze the trigger.

This report did not echo, muffled as it was by the bodies of the two men. The German felt only the punchlike impact and a wetness blossoming from his belly. Still locked in a deadly embrace with the Italian, Wassner felt not pain exactly, just that spreading wet warmth and a wooziness.

Grimacing, Wassner looked into the smiling face of the young Italian, a frozen smile, death-mask smile, the life in the eyes dimming and flickering out. Yanking his gun free of the corpse's grasp, Wassner rolled off the dead sailor and got to his feet, wincing as finally a sharp pain did lance through him, momentarily.

From behind him—just inside the hatchway— came a familiar voice, the black cook's voice, edged with an unfamiliar rage: "Drop it, you Nazi son of a bitch—or don't, and give me an excuse to send you to hell."

Turning, looking up, Wassner was gazing into a glowering black face and down the snout of a Thompson submachine gun.

The German captain, feeling faint, pitched the Luger to the floor. The lowly black cook had him cold.

By the time Tyler got there, breathing hard from his dash down the passageway, it was over. The bloody tableau in the smoky torpedo room told the story: Tank handcuffed to a pipe, discarded fire extinguisher on the floor, Mazzola bleeding on his back from gunshot wounds to the chest, the German standing on shaky legs with his hands up and his belly leaking blood, Eddie training a Thompson on the bastard.

Edging past the mess steward, Tyler grabbed a wrench and inserted it between Tank's cuffs and the pipe, and snapped the chains, leaving the big sailor with silver bracelets and a chagrined expression.

"Jesus, Tank," Tyler said, shaking his head. "One man? You let one man do all this?"

Crossing to the fallen Mazzola, who was staring at nothing, a glazed smile on his lips, Tyler checked the boy's throat for a pulse that he knew would not be there. And he was right. A sick sense of loss flooded through Tyler, and quickly boiled into rage.

"Goddamnit, Tank!"

Barely able to stand, Tank said glumly, "I'm sorry, Mr. Tyler."

Tyler rose from the dead boy and got right in the face of the live one. "Sorry don't cut it, sailor. One man!"

"Nazi skipper's a crafty fucker, sir." Dazed, hurting, Tank touched the red semicircle on his forehead, the indentation of where he'd been slugged by that fire extinguisher, apparently. "I just turned my back for one second and—"

"Secure the diesel." Tyler didn't want to hear excuses or details; he just wanted the show back on the road—right now. "Your prisoner put on a backing bell, Tank, while you were sleeping. And see why the vent valves won't open—today."

"Aye, sir," Tank said, and stumbled into the engine room.

The German looked about to pass out, weaving, groaning from his stomach wound, which he clutched with both hands, red bubbling through.

"Eddie," Tyler said, "get that son of a bitch out of here—he is bleeding on my ship."

"Yes, sir."

"Chain him to a bunk. Get him some goddamn first aid."

The mess steward's expression said that he would rather not; he gestured with the Thompson in his hand. "Couldn't I just give him some of this medicine, Mr. Tyler?"

Wearily, Tyler said, "He's an officer, Eddie. A submarine captain, and a valuable prisoner of war."

Green nodded, sighed. "Aye, aye, sir."

And as the mess steward took the German by the arm, helping him walk, Wassner spat in Green's face. Green just wiped off the spittle, shaking his head, saying, "You *do* wanna get shot, don't ya, Adolf?"

But Wassner had passed out.

"Can you handle him by yourself?" Tyler said.

"Yes, sir. He ain't fakin'. He gives me an excuse, I'm gonna take it."

"Understood."

Tyler was already moving through the engine room, where Tank was carrying out his orders, when over the intercom came Hirsch's distressed voice: "Captain, we have a situation!"

Within moments Tyler was back on the bridge, next to Hirsch and Trigger, the latter on lookout, joining them out in this remarkably beautiful sunny day with its blue sky and blue water, perfection disrupted only by the massive warship that was now broadside, straight off the U-571's bow, a mere two hundred yards away.

"She's getting pretty cozy," Tyler said.

"Take a closer look," Hirsch suggested, handing him the binoculars.

And now Tyler could see quite clearly the Kriegsmarine battle flag streaming from her mast, those devastatingly accurate long-nosed naval guns, the massive deck cannon, a swarm of sailors moving about the lower decks, a scurry of activity on the bridge. None of this was heartening, but worst of all was the sight of a motorboat being lowered into the water—with twelve sailors aboard.

"Christ," Tyler whispered, lowering the binocs; then he called into the voice tube, "Destroyer's sending a launch! Tell Tank to move it!"

Tyler watched through the binoculars as the German sailors unhooked their launch and started up its engine. He handed the glasses to Hirsch.

Up from the hatch came the Chief's voice: "Mr. Tyler—Tank says five minutes!"

"We haven't got five minutes," Tyler yelled back down. "We're a goddamn sinking ship, remember?"

Hirsch, lowering the binocs, said, "Lieutenant, that deck cannon . . ."

"What about it?"

"Could we fire a shell below the waterline and—"

"That wouldn't do a goddamn thing. That barge

could take a hundred shells and just shrug. We need a working torpedo, which we do not have. . . . Trigger!"

"Yes, sir?"

"Man that flak gun. At my command, turn that launch to driftwood."

"Yes, sir."

And the boy climbed down to the deck and took his post at the weapon.

Tyler took back the binoculars and had a look at the German launch, making its way toward them.

Hirsch said, "They're going to find out who we really are in about sixty seconds."

"They're waving, Mr. Hirsch. Let's wave back."

And they did—Tyler keeping an eye on the flak gun Trigger was manning.

From the voice tube came the Chief's voice: "Tank says that son-of-a-bitch German cut off pressure to a manifold. They're searchin' for it, sir!"

Tyler could imagine the maze of pipes they'd be facing back in that compartment, the schematic they'd be trying to make heads or tails of; but he said, "Chief, tell Tank he has one minute. And get Rabbit and Wentz up here on the bridge, and have 'em bring me a Thompson, would you? Trigger, ready that weapon."

"Yes, sir."

The launch with the smiling, waving German sailors was nearing the U-571.

"Mr. Hirsch," Tyler said softly, "what happens when they find out we're not German?"

"After they blow this spy sub out of the water?" Hirsch whispered back bitterly, waving, smiling at the approaching sailors. "They radio to headquarters, and tell them the Enigma's been compromised. Making everything we've done be for nothing."

"They can't if we knock out their radio first."

"What? How in hell?"

"Deck cannon." Tyler nodded toward the warship. "It'd be a doozy of a shot, but suppose we could pull it off. That sure would buy us some time."

"Yeah," Hirsch said, slowly, apparently not sure he was buying this line of reasoning, "but what then? Where does that leave us?"

"We do what subs do: we dive. We get under their ass and lure them in closer to the Continent—in range of Allied air cover."

Hirsch's forehead was frowning, but his lips were smiling, and it wasn't just at the advancing sailors. "And radio in an airstrike?"

"Bingo."

Rabbit and Wentz climbed up out of the hatch onto the bridge. Rabbit had the machine gun Tyler had requested, but was keeping it low, under cover of the bridge railing, surreptitiously handing it to his commander.

Tyler nodded toward their neighbor. "Rabbit, you see that big Nazi destroyer over there?"

Rabbit gulped, eyes huge with the warship. "That one, sir?"

"That one."

"Yes, sir."

"See that structure topside, just aft of the flying bridge?"

"With the big antenna sticking out of it?"

"That's exactly right, Rabbit. With the big antenna sticking out of it. That's the radio shack. You and Wentz get on the deck gun. On my command, you're going to put a shell right through that radio shack's porthole."

"I am, sir?"

"You are."

Rabbit and Wentz traded worried looks, and Tyler snapped, "Don't think about it, do it."

The two sailors swallowed and, no doubt fighting every instinct of self-preservation within them, said in unison, "Aye, aye, sir."

And they climbed down the conning tower ladder to get at the deck gun, just as the motorboat of Germans arrived, its bow nudging the U-571.

Standing in the boat, ready to throw them a line, was a heavyset bosun with a moon face, who yelled up, in German, "Hello, gentlemen! How about a hand tying up these lines?"

The pudgy bosun's pleasant expression shifted as Rabbit and Wentz walked over not to him, to give him the help he'd requested, but to the deck cannon, where Wentz removed the muzzle plug and Rabbit spun handwheels, peering into the gunsight.

And aiming the cannon at the warship.

The bosun's expression had turned to a mingling of shock and fear and—as he looked up at Tyler, placidly standing on the bridge—the bosun shouted something in German to his crew.

"Trigger," Tyler said calmly, "aim at that fat bastard, right there, but don't shoot unless I say so."

"Yes, sir," Trigger said, swinging the flak gun

until its barrel was trained right on the bosun, who looked up at the bridge just in time to see Tyler pointing the Thompson down at him.

Then the bosun, and the other German sailors, stuck their hands in the air—without prompting in any language.

Tyler said, "Hirsch, tell these idiots to go away."

"Go away!" Hirsch yelled.

"Uh . . . try it in German, would you?"

"Sorry," Hirsch said, and flashed a tiny embarrassed smile, then repeated his command in German.

The pudgy bosun—hands high—nodded, obviously grateful to be spared, knowing his unarmed motor launch would be destroyed, otherwise, and he and all his men killed. Sitting back down, throwing the motor in reverse, he backed away, then turned toward the destroyer, starting to cross back.

"Deck gun is manned," Rabbit said, "and ready in all respects, Skipper!"

That was the first time any of his men had called him that.

Tyler was smiling as he said, "Fire!"

Rabbit yanked the firing lever and, with a report that seemed to shake not only the ship but the sea and the sky themselves, sent a shell shrieking toward the destroyer . . .

. . . and punching right through the radio room's armor plating, with a blast so loud, it might have been on the U-571.

But it wasn't: it was the radio shack on that destroyer that had been obliterated.

And as Rabbit and Wentz scurried back up onto

the bridge, Tyler yelled down the hatch: "Dive, Chief! Dive!"

And then the men up top on the U-571—and their skipper—were scrambling down the ladder into the Control Room, while the deck of the destroyer bled smoke into the blue sky.

THE LAST ONE down, Tyler—still on the ladder—slammed the hatch shut after him, spinning the handwheel as the Chief below him spun valves with the precision of a vaudeville juggler twirling plates.

They had to move fast, Tyler knew—they needed to take advantage of the confusion Rabbit's radio-shack shot had no doubt created. On the deck of that destroyer, alarms would be sounding, battle stations called, officers and sailors bumping into each other, bewildered at being fired upon by one of their own U-boats.

"Why aren't we diving?" Tyler demanded, moving to the periscope.

"Tank's still working on those repairs," the Chief said.

"Trigger, take the helm."

"Aye, sir," Trigger said, and did.

Tyler snatched the intercom mike from its perch and said, "Tank, all ahead full! Eddie, we need you up here on the planes with Rabbit."

That the cook would be assigned such an essen-

195

tial and technical task seemed to surprise Hirsch, Tyler noted. The Naval Reserve officer was unaware that every man on a sub had a back-up job, and working the planes was the mess steward's.

Peering through the periscope, at high power, Tyler could make out sailors scrambling on the destroyer's deck, some of them manning machine guns, others the long-nosed deck guns. The radio shack was a charred burning memory.

"Rabbit," Tyler said, "maybe you didn't put one through that porthole, like I asked—but that's damn fine shooting, nevertheless."

"Thank you, sir!"

Nodding at Hirsch, Tyler gestured to the periscope. "Have a look for yourself, Lieutenant."

Hirsch grasped the handles and settled his face into the foam-rubber-rimmed eyepiece. Then he drew away, stunned. "Good God—it's sitting still, but we're charging ahead—plowing right at them!"

"That's the plan."

Hirsch, hands still on the 'scope handles, regarded Tyler with wide eyes. "The plan?"

"Big guns like those can't get us, if we're right under 'em—and machine guns won't faze us, just bullets bouncin' off Superman's chest."

Horrified, Hirsch asked, "Maybe so, but can we dive in time to clear her keel?"

"Let's pray we can, Mr. Hirsch." Tyler lowered the 'scope. "Collision's no more appealing to me than a well-placed Nazi shell."

Eddie Green was seated on the bench at the planes, next to Rabbit—a colored man and a white boy at the controls of a U-boat, Tyler thought with a smile. That had to be a first.

Bullets began slamming into the iron skin of the sub—machine-gun fire pelting the boat, like a torrent of hailstones, and about as deadly. Right now those big gun turrets would be swinging ominously onto the renegade U-boat; but those turrets would not be able to depress low enough to fire on the U-571.

In the rear torpedo room, Tank also could hear the battering of bullets on the sub, dinging and pinging, but he ignored it as he opened a wall locker, even though the sound grew louder, closer to the hull as he was. Shining a flashlight on the exposed valves, poking in his head, and spotting just the valves he was after, Tank grinned and said, "Gotcha!"

As he turned the wheels, the dinging of bullets seemed to increase, as if the Germans knew he'd been successful.

Then he moved to the nearest voice tube and reported proudly: "Hydraulics shifted to Control!"

In the Control Room, Tyler spoke into his intercom mike. "Good job, Tank! That did the trick—we're going down."

"Uh, Captain," Tank said, "we got a grinding noise out of the starboard E-motor."

"What's the problem?"

"I don't know, sir. It don't sound pretty."

"Well, get on it."

"Aye, sir."

The ship was submerging, only the conning tower still exposed—the pinging of fire from MP-

4Os like a shooting gallery above the Control Room crew—and even without the 'scope to look through, Tyler knew his boat was dead smack in front of the destroyer, at the moment the U-571 dipped under the waves. Bracing himself for collision, half-expecting to scrape the warship's keel, Tyler waited, and waited, as did every man around him.

"We're clear," the Chief said finally, eyes on the depth gauge.

Smiles and sighs of relief blossomed around Tyler, who was gazing up, where the rumble of boilers, growing ever louder, signaled the destroyer's new strategy. Right now the massive twin screws, several tons of hand-finished bronze, sat stone-still in the waters as the U-571 glided under the warship. But those boilers kicking in told Tyler this was temporary: and he was right.

Clutches were engaged.

Screws began spinning to life, churning water in opposite directions.

Wentz, on the hydrophones, called out, "The destroyer's turnin' around, Captain!"

Tyler felt a chill. Despite its size, a destroyer like that could be a lithe and agile hunter, lunging after its prey. Once that ship had turned to come after the U-571, those massive screws would work together, pushing her forward, churning water furiously.

He knew what was next. He hoped his men were ready. He hoped he was ready.

"Fifty meters," the Chief said.

"Destroyer maneuvering," Wentz said from the

radio room through the hatchway. "Really chewing up water, Captain. . . . Splashes!"

Hirsch's eyes were wide again. "Splashes? What—"

"Goddamn ash cans," Klough said.

Still confused, Hirsch asked Tyler, "Ash cans?"

Wentz called: "More splashes!"

"Depth charges," Tyler said.

They would have racks of the damn things up on that destroyer, on the aft deck; even as he and his men waited for the inevitable explosions, Tyler knew German sailors were preparing the next round, screwing in fuses, setting depth with a special key, dumping the fat barrels over the stern, like gangsters disposing of bodies.

"Ever been ash-canned, Chief?" Rabbit asked lightly, eyes terrified, seated next to Green, who sat on his bench calm as a churchgoer on a pew.

"Sure I have." Klough was gazing up—not toward God, either. "Worst was in the Great War, off Murmansk. Krauts gave us a hell of a shellacking. One of them cans came so close it knocked four teeth out of the skipper's head."

"Did . . . did anybody die?"

"Hell, yes, Rabbit! It killed me dead! Can't you tell?"

Deathly pale, watching the ceiling, Hirsch clutched a pipe, holding on with both white-knuckled hands, like a subway rider gripping a pole.

"Mr. Hirsch," Tyler said, "step away from that bulkhead. The shock wave can snap a man's spine."

Hirsch let go, as if the pipes had gone red-hot.

An explosion—like underwater cannonfire—sent a tremor through the ship; then another—a bit louder—made the boat tremble.

But the one-two punch made Tyler—and every man in the Control Room—jump, *twice*, as none of them had been through this before, except in simulation back at New London sub school.

Every man except the Chief, that is, who looked with faint disgust at the jumpy souls around him, saying dismissively, "That wasn't even close. You girls ain't seen nothin' yet."

The boys around him were saucer-eyed, staring at the ceiling, except for the cringing Hirsch, whose head was lowered.

"Left full rudder," Tyler said. He reached for the mike, spoke into it: "Tank—all back."

In the rear torpedo room, Tank—at the motor control panel—hit the appropriate breakers and switches, but the effect was not the desired one: sparks and smoke shot out in a tiny, nasty fireworks display. The E-motors stopped, and reversed, the starboard E-motor freezing up, a breaker snapping open with another Fourth of July burst of sparks.

Moments later, in the Control Room, Tank's sorry report came breathlessly out of the voice tube: "Captain, that starboard E-motor that was grinding—it's out of commission now. That goddamn German must've sabotaged it!"

"Can you fix it, fast?"

"I can't fix it, slow, sir—it's fuckin' fried."

"Goddamnit!" Tyler said, and put the mike back.

"No way we'll make Allied air cover creeping along on one lousy motor."

But he immediately knew he shouldn't have voiced this concern aloud, as expressions of worry and gloom popped up all around the Control Room. Dahlgren would have kept that to himself.

"Splashes, sir!" Wentz called through the hatchway. "Lots more splashes!"

"Oh, shit," Klough said softly.

"*How* many?" Tyler asked Wentz.

"Lost count, sir."

Tyler frowned in thought. "They must be charging straight ahead, dumping ash cans in a line. . . . Okay!"

And Tyler issued commands, designed to sidestep out from under the depth charges, like a boxer deftly ducking punches. The U-571 slowed, stopped, began creeping backward, with a single screw spinning, turning, gliding out of the path of the ash cans.

The direct path, anyway.

And the ash cans detonated, in a sound familiar only to Klough but soon all too familiar to every man on the U-571: *klik, boom!* . . .

Lightbulbs exploded, paint flaked from the overhead, cork hull-lining rained down . . .

. . . *klik, boom!* . . .

. . . a locker flew open and flung gear across the Control Room . . .

. . . *klik, boom!* . . .

. . . men were hurled from their posts and thrown against bulkheads . . .

. . . *klik, boom!* . . .

. . . in the rear torpedo room, Tank was tossed between bulkheads like a tennis ball careening off two surfaces . . .

. . . *klik, boom!* . . .

. . . dishes and foodstuffs flew from cabinets and crashed against bulkheads and onto the deck . . .

. . . *klik, boom!* . . .

. . . the phongraph in the radio room leapt from its brackets, past a startled Wentz, and smashed to the floor, shelving collapsing, 78s pitching to the floor, shattering . . .

. . . *klik, boom!* . . .

. . . in the crew quarters, Kapitanlieutnant Wassner, his belly bandaged, hands cuffed, was buffeted around in his bunk, the jostling rousing him to wakefulness.

Then the rain of underwater bombshells ceased, as abruptly as it had begun. In darkness now, a few hands found flashlights and beams stroked across frightened faces; one of those beams found Tyler, as he plucked glass and bits of cork from his hair.

"Chief," Tyler said, "get us a good trim."

"Aye, sir. We're at one hundred meters, sir."

"Hold us there." Tyler found the intercom mike and used it: "Tank, ahead two-thirds."

"Aye, sir," came Tank's voice from the tube.

"Eddie, see if you can find some lightbulbs that survived that salvo."

"Yes, sir."

As the mess steward moved through the hatchway, Tyler followed along for a moment, to peer out at Wentz, in the hydrophone room, like a veteran safecracker as he turned a handwheel on a console with a delicate touch and listened at his headphones with intense concentration.

"Report, Mr. Wentz."

"Nothing, sir . . . nothing. . . . Mr. Tyler! Destroyer . . ."

"Yes? Yes?"

"Destroyer closing, sir!"

Soon they could hear the warship for themselves: the hum of its boilers, the gallop of her screws, growing closer, closer, ever closer. . . .

Mess Steward Green came back with an armload of lightbulbs; he and the Chief screwed them in, providing illumination but scant comfort.

Into the intercom mike, Tyler asked, "Tank, can you fix the stern tube?"

From the voice tube came Tank's wary reply: "I don't know, Mr. Tyler."

" 'I don't know' is not what I'm looking for, Tank. Yes or no—can you repair that goddamn torpedo tube?"

"Yes, sir, I'll fix the SOB, sir."

"Good man." He replaced the mike, turned to Klough. "Chief, make your depth one six zero meters."

The Chief winced, turning his head sideways: that was more than five hundred feet; and they both knew what that meant.

"Think this pig can take that, sir?" Klough asked, lightly enough, helping Tyler out by not letting the others know the extent of his concern.

Tyler nodded and pointed down.

Nodding back, the Chief said, "Aye, sir, one six zero meters. Twenty degrees dive both planes."

"Twenty degrees dive, Chief, aye," Green said. The mess steward glanced over at Tyler, leaning against the periscope. "Sir, you by any chance considerin' goin' up against that destroyer with one fish and a busted motor?"

"Way past considering it, Eddie," Tyler said. "It's exactly what we're going to do."

Hirsch, looking pale and sick, said, "How wise is that?"

"Probably about as wise as dressing up like Nazis and taking over a U-boat. Mr. Hirsch, come here a minute."

Tyler grabbed the deck log from the chart table, and a pencil, and as Hirsch fell in alongside him, Tyler began to draw a diagram.

"There is no way a two-knot submarine can get in firing position against a thirty-knot destroyer," Tyler said.

"Agreed."

"Or is there? Suppose we go deep, and shoot all that junk we already have loaded up in the forward tubes, blow it out into the ocean, letting our friends up top think their ash cans did us in."

"Will they buy that? After we faked that fire?"

"What choice will they have? They'll be in the middle of a debris field. The commander will have to maneuver to the center of it, shut down his engines, to make things nice and quiet, and do an acoustic search to make goddamn good and sure we really are dead."

"But we're not."

"Not yet we aren't, Mr. Hirsch. We're here"—Tyler drew a rising arrow—"on our way to periscope depth. In case they omitted this at reserve officer's training, let me point out a principle of ascent velocity: we let our buoyancy pull us up—and away—from that destroyer, opening up the range some. By the time we get to periscope depth, Mr. Hirsch, we'll be showing that warship our rusty ass from a good seven hundred yards."

"And that's a good thing, Mr. Tyler?"

"Real good. A perfect position for a stern shot on a stationary target."

Hirsch looked at Tyler like he was seeing him for the first time. "That's a hell of a plan . . . Captain."

The Chief, who'd been eavesdropping—and every man in the Control Room had heard this speech, and was clearly impressed—said, "That's awful pretty, Skipper."

"Don't come much prettier, Chief."

Nodding to his depth gauge, the Chief said, "Passing one two zero meters, sir."

"Very well. Rabbit, load Mazzola's body in tube three. Put an escape rig on him so he floats."

The faces around Tyler, which had lit up with new hope for their situation, and new respect for him, darkened instantly.

Still seated on his bench at the planes, Rabbit said, "Mr. Tyler—we're gonna shoot Mazzola out like . . . garbage?"

"I'd rather see him buried with honors on American soil," Tyler said somberly, "but I think he'd want to help keep all of us from dying down here. A dead body floating in that debris makes it look like they really got us. Load him up."

Sighs and nods of resignation around Tyler told him that the boys knew this was the right—if regrettable—thing to do.

Rabbit swallowed. "Mind if I say a few words over him, first, Mr. Tyler?"

"Send him along with all our prayers, Mr. Parker."

And Rabbit rose from the planes and headed aft.

"Eddie," Tyler said, "you'll have to handle both planes."

"Yes, sir, I got 'em, sir."

The Chief said, "Passing one three zero meters, Skipper."

Suddenly Hirsch was right beside him, whispering in Tyler's ear. "A word with you . . ."

Tyler stepped to one side with Hirsch, whose expression was grave.

"Mr. Tyler," Hirsch said quietly, so quietly no one but Tyler could hear him, "if you can't take out that destroyer, the danger is not that some of us may die—it's that some of us may live."

"Explain."

Hirsch nodded toward the boys in the Control Room. "These men have seen and heard things that must not be revealed to the enemy. Secrets such as our radar capabilities, not to mention our understanding of enemy encryption. If we fall into German hands, we will be tortured without mercy."

Tyler said nothing.

"Mr. Tyler, I'm not a brave man—you can see for yourself, all of this is new to me, and I only hope I have been more a help than a hindrance."

"Mr. Hirsch, you've proven yourself again and again."

"Thank you, Captain. I appreciate that. I sense that . . . we have earned each other's respect. But I won't lie to you: I fear death, and dying down here is . . . well, we'll do what we have to do, won't we, Mr. Tyler, for this great effort, for our country."

"Of course."

"What I'm trying to say, in my clumsy way, is that capture would be worse than death. You must either succeed in sinking that destroyer or you must see to it that none of us survive."

And Hirsch stepped away from him, leaving Tyler to contemplate the faces of the boys around him, and for the first time fully understand what Captain Dahlgren had meant about hard decisions, and asking men to carry out orders that might result in their death.

16

AS THE U-571 slipped farther down into the ocean, slinking into the darkness of the deep, Tyler glanced up, swearing he could sense the hull of the destroyer gliding overhead.

From the radio room, Wentz—his hydrophone headset reporting the screw sounds—confirmed his skipper's sensation: "Passing over us, Captain."

Tyler smiled. Despite their dire situation, he felt a coolness, a confidence: he knew his foe. The Americans on the commandeered U-boat might not know the name of the opposing ship, but Tyler could picture in his mind's eye the activity on her decks, men poised at weapons, the Kriegsmarine officers on the bridge talking tactics over a chart, sailors using a small crane to load fresh depth charges into racks as others fused them, and set detonation depth. The cat-and-mouse game of destroyer and sub was an old, familiar one, and the strategy followed by the commander of either hinged little, if at all, on whether he wore an American or German uniform—a point underscored by the German uniform Tyler wore right now.

Still cleaning up after the depth charge barrage, the Chief was screwing in one last lightbulb, as Rabbit and Hirsch came up from aft, marching somberly through the Control Room as they hauled the limp body of their fellow crewman, Anthony Mazzola, who would never see Brooklyn again.

The sight of the pale corpse, chest blackened by the scorch of close-range pistol fire and caked, dried blood, was a sobering one for Tyler and the boys around him. Tyler's tiny confident smile vanished as Rabbit—walking backward, his arms under the dead sailor's shoulders—shot his commander a reproving look.

Tyler could hardly blame the boy—it would be hard to imagine a more horrible job than the one he'd assigned Rabbit and Hirsch.

The two reluctant pallbearers slipped through the hatch, moving forward with their ghastly cargo.

"Mr. Tyler!" Wentz called from the radio room, moments after the grim procession had passed his post. "Destroyer is zigzagging! Splashes— splashes—more splashes. They're dropping a hell of a lot of ash cans, sir."

Tyler gazed up, almost admiringly; the commander of that warship was a wily old salt. "He's dropping a box pattern on us. Tank, line up to pump the engine room bilge to sea. Rabbit, stand by to fire the tubes!"

In the forward torpedo room, Rabbit was just closing the breech door of tube four.

The young torpedoman swallowed, glancing at Hirsch, nodding to the reserve lieutenant to bow his head, which the bookish officer did.

"We commend thy soul to God," Rabbit said softly, "and commit thy body to the deep."

"Amen," Hirsch said.

From the intercom came Tyler's voice: "Fire those tubes!"

Rabbit slammed a fist on one, then the other firing valve.

"So long, Mazzola," he said.

The familiar sound—*ka-thunk!*—reverberated once, twice, three times, and four as high-pressure air propelled the debris out of the sub with a bubbling hiss.

Propelled by these four geysers, debris drifted toward the surface, where a shirt popped up, then a pillow, a few empty jars, then a soggy loaf of bread, and a glove, now several dirty French magazines, whose covers bore ooo-la-la girls showing leg, here postcards riding the froth, there a mattress, and many, many life preservers, worn by no one, bobbing in a serene ballet of rubbish, the star performer one Anthony Mazzola, performing a hollow-eyed pirouette.

The crew of the U-571 was not an audience for this performance; they were on their way into the depths, the sub's drain pump outlet seeping a steady stream of oil, bubbles of liquid obsidian rising even as the ship sought waters almost as black as that oil itself.

Rabbit and Hirsch shuffled back in the Control Room, the torpedoman's shoulders slumping as he took his position next to the mess steward on the planes.

Tyler went to the boy, put a supportive hand on

his shoulder, saying of Mazzola, "He's doing us a service," but Rabbit just looked away.

"It's coming," Tyler said to everyone, referring to the depth charges that he knew even now were floating downward. "We survived the first round. We'll do it again—this deep, we'll have an advantage. Brace yourselves."

The crew waited in nervous anticipation—some were praying, all were sweating, taking quick, quiet breaths, listening, listening, listening, for that awful combination of sounds. . . .

. . . *Klik, boom!*

Distant sounding.

A big smile blossomed in Eddie Green's face. "We're gonna be all right."

"Pretty far away," Tyler granted.

. . . *klik, boom!* . . .

. . . a little closer . . .

. . . *klik, boom!* . . .

. . . closer . . .

. . . *klik, boom!* . . .

. . . much closer, ship reverberating now . . .

. . . *klik, boom!* . . .

. . . rocking now, riding rough, like a Ford going sixty blowing a tire . . .

. . . *klik, boom!* . . .

. . . in the rear torpedo room, the massive Tank was knocked to the floor like a Coke bottle . . .

. . . *klik, boom!* . . .

. . . way too fucking close! Those new lightbulbs popped like glass pimples. The Chief hit a switch and the night-running lights came up, suffusing the startled sailors with a sick red glow . . .

. . . *klik, boom!* . . .

. . . shaking the ship, but not as close . . .

. . . *klik, boom!* . . .

. . . just a tremor through the ship this time, the explosions receding now . . .

. . . *klik, boom!* . . .

. . . not even a shimmy from the ship from that one—smiles bloomed in their red-tinged world . . .

. . . *klik, boom!* . . .

. . . was that one closer? . . .

. . . *klik, boom!* . . .

. . . oh God, the ship shivered that time . . .

. . . *klik, boom!* . . .

. . . the boat heaved and men tumbled from their posts . . .

. . . *klik, boom!* . . .

. . . frightened faces as men rolled on the deck . . .

. . . *klik, BOOOOOM!* . . .

. . . the big one: right overhead, close as an ash can could come without a direct hit and the glass faces of gauges cracked like the world's ugliest woman had looked at all of them at once and bolts popped loose and shot around the Control Room like wild zinging bullets and the red lighting winked out as shock waves reverberated through the boat in a deafening din, like the sub was a big steel drum and God was banging on it!

A huge goddamn snake was hissing—or was that air from a broken pipe? Arcs and sparks strobed from a breaker panel, giving an appearance of movement to the crew, who were actually frozen at or near their posts, the only real motion spraying water from stray leaks.

"Am I dead?" Rabbit asked, hanging onto his planes bench.

"Maybe," Trigger said, crawling back up to the helm controls. "But then so am I, and I guess we sinned, 'cause this sure feels like hell."

"Fuck a duck!" the Chief said, grinning crazily, getting to his feet. "That mamma was close! Went off right over our heads."

"Bet there's some little fishies with earaches out there," Green said, back on the planes.

Tyler said, "Secure that air leak, Chief."

Klough found himself a battle lantern and, in its dim light, traced the hissing to an air valve and closed it off.

Now the boat was quiet—eerily so. They could hear themselves and each other breathe—and they could hear the boat breathe too, creaking and groaning under the pressure of their continued descent.

"What's our depth, Chief?" Tyler asked Klough.
Klik!

Everybody jumped, including Tyler—everybody but Klough, that is, who had just clicked on a flashlight.

"Don't wet your panties, ladies," the Chief chuckled. He pointed the flashlight beam at the cracked face of the depth gauge. "One six zero meters—we are at your ordered depth, sir." Then to Green and Rabbit, Klough said, "Zero the planes."

Tyler was screwing in a new fuse at a panel, and the red night-running lights came back on, the lights within gauges coming alive, too. The crimson flush of the lighting revealed a Control Room littered with broken glass, flaked-off paint, cork, insulation scraps, and flung gear and tools and charts and—hell, Control was a goddamn mess. Could not be worse.

"Splashes!" Wentz called out. "More splashes, way too close together to count!"

Cursing under his breath, Tyler gazed around the Control Room, thinking it through, making one of those hard decisions Dahlgren had promised him this job would bring.

He said, "Chief, make your depth two hundred meters. We're gonna get under those damn things if it kills us."

"It . . . it might, sir," the Chief said. The veteran sailor had wide eyes and a troubled expression, and had stepped away from his depth gauge, shaking his head, no.

As the boys around them traded looks, Tyler got in Klough's face. "We will not break into discussion groups. I have given you a lawful order and, goddamnit, I expect you to carry it out. Two hundred meters, Chief. Do it."

The Chief's eyes narrowed, and he backed away from his skipper, returning to his post.

"Aye, sir," Klough said. "Making my depth two hundred meters." He turned to the two men at the planes. "Rabbit, Eddie—ten degrees dive both planes."

Rabbit and the mess steward complied.

Soon all eyes were on the depth gauge, whose needle began its inexorable journey into the red.

Tyler said into the intercom mike, "Tank, report on that after torpedo tube."

From the voice tube came Tank's response: "Couple, two, three things wrong, but we're getting there. Muzzle door is operable, now. Working on the impulse air, right now."

As the boat nosed into the depths, and that gauge needle dug deeper into the red, the hull complained, creaking and whining and moaning. The U-571 seemed suddenly a haunted house, Tyler and his men the ghosts haunting it.

"Passing one eight zero meters," the Chief said.

From the voice tube came alarmed, agitated words from Tank: "Mr. Tyler, my depth gauge back here says a hundred and eighty meters!"

"Thank you, Tank," Tyler replied into the intercom mike.

"Well, Jesus, sir, I just thought you should know."

"We'd noticed. Back to work."

"Aye, sir."

Small, though powerful streams of water began to shoot in, here and there, like pinpricks in a balloon letting out streams of air. From somewhere in the piping came a ticking, a clicking, unidentifiable but there, ominously so. The Chief's eyes followed the pipes, as if he hoped to trace the sound, shaking his head as he did.

Tyler moved under a spray of water, like a man at a shower head, letting it stream coldly over his upturned face. He had to keep his stress hidden; both he *and* this tub had to hold up under the pressure.

"Two hundred meters, Lieutenant," Klough said. "Eddie, Rabbit—stay on top of those planes!"

Tyler glanced at the sweeping second hand on his wristwatch. The commander of that destroyer should be responding to that debris field by now— Mazzola's body and that debris should be in sight . . .

. . . and they were, though Tyler couldn't know that, could only hope and pray that it was so.

But it was so: Mazzola's life-jacketed body bobbed on the surface, dead eyes staring up at a sun he would never see again, rubbish floating around him, oil pooling slickly.

A lookout on the destroyer sighted the debris field, shouted into a voice tube and soon the destroyer—whose name was *Anschluss*—had taken Tyler's bait; an officer barked orders, the helmsman spinning the wheel, the warship swinging to port, moving toward what appeared to be the aftermath of the renegade U-boat's demise by depth charge.

That U-boat was still alive, however, creeping slowly along at an ungodly depth, awaiting the arrival of the next batch of ash cans.

Klik, boom! . . . boom . . . boom . . . boom . . . boom!

The depth charges thudded above them like a bass drum, the ship reverberating, but no lightbulbs popping, no sailors tossed like kittens, no shower of cork particles or paint flakes or flying plates— just a trembling, like their own trembling, in the red-tinged world of the Control Room.

Seconds slipped by, and no more explosions, only a silence broken by the occasional creak or squeak from the bitchy hull, and that *tick-tick-tick*ing in the pipes.

The Chief was beaming at the overhead, holding his palms out, catching some water spray like a farmer delighted a drought had ended. "Jesus, Mary and Joseph, but those Krauts can build a boat. All the goddamn ash cans in the world dropped on us, and they didn't do diddly squat."

Tyler was beaming, too.

Then the ticking in the pipes accelerated, and suddenly ruptured in a *whoosh* that signaled a major piping system giving way, down at the after end of Control.

"Jesus!" Klough cried.

Seawater was rushing in now, roaring into the boat, no tiny pinprick sprays, but a violent gush, flooding in like a dam had burst. Tyler had never seen the like of it in his days as a submariner, and—if he lived through this—hoped never to, again.

"Take her up, Chief!" Tyler said. "Take her up now!"

"Blowing negative!" Klough said. "Planes full rise!"

"Rabbit," Tyler said, "see if you can isolate that leak."

Seawater washed across the deck plates, as Rabbit left the planes bench to slosh to that "leak," rather that wall of rushing water, a man trying to walk into the stream of a full-blast firehose.

"You seein' this, Chief?" a horrified Green asked Klough.

"Fuckin' needle's off the scale!" the Chief said,

eyeing the depth gauge. "We have to blow main ballast tanks!"

Around Tyler was a disaster in progress, a break panel arcing and sparking, flames licking up from decking in the after part of Control. The sound of fire cracking in one ear, and of surging water in the other, Tyler said, "Blow main ballast tanks!"

The Chief released the blow valves, adding the hiss of air to the symphony of sounds in the beleaguered Control Room. The ballast tank sight glasses revealed water being slowly pushed out. But Rabbit was struggling with a large, heavy valve, as fire snapped, and the flooding continued, unabated.

And the depth gauge needle was pointing straight down.

"Mr. Tyler," Klough said, "securing high pressure blow. Ballast tanks are bone-dry and yet we're *still* going down!"

At that stuck valve wheel, Rabbit—veins popping on his forehead—cried over the roar of rushing water, "I can't budge this bastard!"

Tyler sloshed over to help Rabbit, latching onto the big wheel, putting everything he had in it—and yet, even straining together, the two men couldn't force the goddamn thing!

Then someone wedged in a crowbar, across the valve wheel—Tank.

Tyler nodded to the machinist mate and Tank nodded back to his skipper as all three men latched onto that crowbar and tugged down, and down— the wheel still refusing to turn, and the crowbar bending!

But just as Tyler and Tank were trading unbelieving looks, the valve gave way, and Rabbit quickly spun it closed.

The water flow diminished, then stopped.

Tyler, Tank and Rabbit stood there, ankle deep in water, chests heaving.

From over by the depth gauge, Green called out: "Two hundred meters and rising!"

Still trying to catch their breath, Tyler and the two sailors stood smiling at each other, appreciating this good news.

Then the Chief was next to them, saying, "Mr. Tyler, we *are* coming up, sir—but I've lost control of the ballast tanks."

And this was bad news: that meant the Chief could not stop or control their ascent. They were on their way up, and that was that.

"Tank," Tyler said to the machinist mate, "where are we with that stern torpedo?"

"Piping's damaged," Tank said, shaking his head woefully, jerking a thumb, aft. "There's a break in the damn air line."

"No pressure to launch a torpedo?"

"No pressure, sir. I tried to bypass the leak, but it's way back in the bilge. There's no way I can get back down in there, to reach it." He gestured to his bulky frame. "I just can't fit!"

Tyler's eyes narrowed. "But somebody smaller *could?*"

"Maybe." Tank shrugged. "Pretty goddamn dangerous, Skipper. Whoever tries this could get stuck back there . . . and, well, drown."

"We're all going to drown, or get blown to shit,"

Tyler said, with a glance at the Chief, "if we don't try this."

Klough was already sizing up their crew. "You need a pee-wee for this job. That makes it Rabbit or Trigger."

"I know," Tyler said, looking over at Rabbit on the planes, Trigger on the helm, the two youngest boys of all the boys of the S-33 and, now, the U-571.

This was another of those terrible choices, those hard decisions Dahlgren had warned him about. *Be careful what you wish for*, his skipper's voice said, reverberating in his mind like his skull had been depth-charged.

Green, at the depth gauge, said, "One hundred ninety-five meters."

"Sir," the Chief said quietly, but insistently, "you gotta pick one. Choose."

Tyler swallowed, composed himself. Then he called out, "Trigger! Got a job for you. Lay aft with Tank."

Trigger winced. Like everyone here, he'd heard all that had been said, and knew what being assigned this "job" meant. The boy looked around at the other faces, including that of Rabbit, as if he were thinking of saying, "I think *he's* a little smaller than me, sir."

But Trigger didn't say that.

The Chief said, "Shake a leg, son."

Swallowing, Trigger rose and followed Tank, aft.

"Sir!" Wentz called from the hydrophone shack. Tyler went over to the hatchway, bent down to where he could see Wentz, who was listening carefully, eyes closed, as if meditating, pressing the headphone to his ear.

Softly, Wentz said, "I can hear her. She's making slow turns . . . just stopped her screws! I think they've seen the debris. . . . Sir, I think maybe they're buying it!"

The Chief said, "One eight zero meters, Skipper."

Tyler moved back into the Control Room, wading through the remaining water, saying, "Slow our ascent, some."

"No can do, sir."

"*Please,* Chief."

"Sorry, Mr. Tyler. No discussion on this, either— out of our hands. We got a one-way ticket topside."

Tyler glanced over at the depth gauge, whose needle had arced into the yellow.

"We surface without a torpedo to fire," Tyler said, "that leaves us one option."

"Yeah?" Klough asked, not knowing of one.

"We'll make a swell target."

And the U-571 continued its upward journey, leaving the inky waters behind, seeking sunshine.

IN THE REAR torpedo room, Tank removed the key deck plates, giving access to the bilge, and gave Trigger a hand, helping the diminutive sailor as he climbed down into that foul, dark wet recess.

Water up to his waist, Trigger—the top third of him visible as he stood in the hole the removed deck plates had left—said, "It's cold!"

Tank crouched beside him, showing him a chart—the words were in German, but the pictures could be read by any submariner. "Just follow these pipes," the big machinist mate said, pointing, tracing along. "That right there is the pressure gauge."

"Next to the torpedo tank."

"Yeah, exactly right. Right now we got no air pressure to fire that fish. One of these pipes *has* to be busted, and leakin' air."

"How am I supposed to find it down there? It's darker than dogshit!"

"Watch for the bubbles comin' out. Should be a mess of 'em. You'll find the isolation valve *aft* of the leak, then just crank it down."

Teeth chattering, the boy nodded. "Crank it down."

"Got all that?"

"Aft of the leak. Got it."

"Okay. Just a second . . ." Tank went over and got Trigger a Dreager rebreather, which he'd attached to a seemingly endless length of rubber hose running to a compressor. Tank handed the gear to Trigger who, with a world-weary sigh that belied his young age, bit down on the mouthpiece, and attached the nose clip.

"Soon as you crank it down," Tank said, a hand on the boy's shoulder, "you haul ass outa there. You don't wanna be near those valves when the torpedo fires. You hear me?"

Eyes hooded, Trigger nodded, and slipped down into the oily bilgewater.

Swimming down under, not used to the cold yet, Trigger watched for bubbles—the rebreather, which recycled exhaust air, helped minimize the bubbles he was creating himself—and soon he had spotted a valve leaking air, which he paddled over to and cranked shut.

But as those bubbles ceased, another, more serious stream of bubbles became apparent, seething out from somewhere in the far aft section of the compartment. Feeling very alone in his dark iron-walled world, Trigger stroked under water, toward the leak, moving swiftly—until his air hose yanked him back!

He tugged at it, but he was at the end of the line, literally.

Tank, waiting above, kneeling at the opening in the deck plates, heard Trigger's voice, from elsewhere in the torpedo compartment.

"Hey! Over here!"

Tank hustled over to a grate amid the deck plates and saw Trigger down there, looking up, soaked to the skin, mouthpiece spit aside. Tank shone a flashlight down on the frantic face visible through the hatchwork.

"I . . . I got . . . one of 'em." The boy was breathless and his teeth were chattering.

Tank frowned down at Trigger. "There's more than one leak?"

"A-another, yeah, way . . . way the hell . . . back there. Gimme some more slack on that hose."

"I don't have any more to give, buddy."

"Shit. Fuck."

"You gotta grab another big breath and go back down."

"I . . . I know."

And, with a roll of his eyes, removing the rebreather, Ted "Trigger" Fitzgerald dipped back under the nasty brown water, to do his duty.

In the Control Room, Chief Klough was doing his, eyes scanning gauges, looking for the first sign of technical trouble. "One zero five meters, sir."

Tyler checked his watch, trying not to fidget, frustrated by having his ship taken from his hands, by capricious fate and mechanical failure, knowing there was nothing left to do now but wait, and hope the boy swimming down in the bilge was able to make that repair.

Around him, his crew sweated and sighed and squirmed, from time to time closing their eyes, as if hoping, upon opening them, to discover this had all been a bad dream. Wiping streaks of sweat from his face, Rabbit kept his eyes open, fixed upon the compass, making small adjustments to the rudder.

"Beachwood," Hirsch said softly, as if in a reverie.

Tyler blinked and turned to the Naval Reserve officer, whose eyes were distant behind the wire-frames. "What?"

Hirsch twitched half a smile. "Nothing. Just a park I used to go as a kid . . . played ball there. . . . Don't know why the hell I thought of it, now."

Tyler said nothing. But he wondered if the rest of his crew weren't mentally sorting through their own memory books, gazing at faces of friends and families, of their wives or girls, sons and daughters in some cases, saying quiet good-byes.

"One four zero meters," the Chief said, eyes on the depth gauge.

From somewhere came a faint but distinct sound, disrupting the silence—not unlike the ticking that had preceded the burst pipe, earlier, not a ticking, this time, though—more a . . . tapping.

Tyler frowned, glancing around, as others in the Control Room reacted similarly. Was there a pattern to that clicking?

"That's not mechanical," Tyler said.

From the hydrophone shack, Wentz called, "Sir! I can hear it in my headphones. It's Morse code."

As the crew shrugged and traded puzzled expressions, the tapping continuing in its strangely rhythmic fashion, Tyler moved quickly to the hatchway, where he could see Wentz.

Bewildered, Tyler said to the radioman, "What the hell is it? Is that destroyer trying to signal us?"

"I don't think so," Wentz said, frowning. "I think it's . . ."

Tyler did not see the sudden look of panic overtake Hirsch, who'd been concentrating, listening to the tapping.

"Wentz," Tyler said, his back to Hirsch, "what the hell's it saying?"

"Sir," Wentz replied, eyes wide, his expression sickly, "that's coming from *inside* the ship. *I'm alive. Destroy me.*"

Tyler whirled, just as Hirsch—teeth bared, like an angry animal—was grabbing a pipe wrench and ducking through the aft hatchway, on the run.

Ankles bound, hands cuffed, Kapitanlieutnant Gunthar Wassner lay seemingly helpless, weak as kitten, in a curtained bunk in the crew quarters near the galley. He knew he would probably be dead, soon. His stomach was a bloody mess tightly bound with bandages courtesy of that black cook. The pain veered between dull and sharp, depending on the motion of the ship—during the depth charge barrage, he had experienced agony unlike any he'd ever known.

But those depth charges had also done him a great service: they had wakened him, not only to pain, but to an alertness that allowed the captain of the U-571 to continue to serve his hijacked boat, his murdered crew and his beloved country.

Wassner knew the Americans had done their best to convince the destroyer up there that the U-571 had sunk, that the ship was dead. He had deduced, as well, that this callow Tyler intended to use the boat's final torpedo for a sneak attack on the out-foxed warship.

So Captain Wassner determined to send his countrymen a message. Using the chains of his handcuffs, he began to tap on a nearby pipe, sending a succinct signal: "I am alive. Destroy me." He had also initially tapped, "I am Captain Wassner," but soon simplified it. Just the basics: the ship had not sunk, and needed to be.

I am alive. Destroy me.

He had tapped the message six times when the curtain ripped back and the contorted face of the professorial American, Hirsch, hovered over him; tight in the man's upraised right hand was a massive wrench.

"I got your message," Hirsch said in German. "Happy to oblige."

And the wrench swung down.

The last sound Kapitanlieutnant Gunthar Wassner heard was that of his own skull caving in.

With no air supply save what he'd sucked into his lungs before dipping below the mucky surface, Trigger swam deeper, into the far aft compartment, desperately navigating as best he could through a claustrophobic maze of pipes and cables. Small as he was, getting caught there, wedged, was a real risk, and several times he was slowed by temporary entanglements.

But he kept working his way through the piping, until he reached the point where the bubbles were boiling out, and he saw the valve, stretched his fingers through the nest of pipes to get at it, even touched it—but barely. His air was almost gone, and the water in the bilge compartment was rising.

He could not get his hand on the damn thing, let alone try to twist it shut!

Lungs close to bursting, he swam back out through the maze, hoping against hope he wouldn't get entrapped or black out before he could reach the opening in the deck plates.

In the Control Room, where the tapping sound in the pipes had ceased, Tyler and everybody else looked up as Hirsch—moving slowly now, almost zombielike—stumbled back in, the wrench no longer in his hand.

Dazed, blood flecking his cheek like red teardrops, Hirsch met Tyler's gaze with a shrug. "We had one captain too many."

Tyler nodded his approval.

Eddie Green said to Hirsch, "Got a little somethin' there, sir," pointing to his own cheek, and the Naval Reserve lieutenant wiped his face with the sleeve of his Kriegsmarine uniform.

The Chief said, "Mr. Tyler—coming up on ninety meters."

From the hydrophone room, Wentz called out: "Engines starting—screws turning!"

Tyler went over to the hatchway. "You think they've heard us, Mr. Wentz?"

As if in reply, ominous *pings* reverberated through the Control Room—this was no signal from a Nazi prisoner, rather the ominous signature of the destroyer's ASDIC sonar.

"I've got sonar pings," Wentz said, not realizing

everyone in Control was hearing the same thing he was, in his headphones. "They've seen us, sir."

Tyler knew the destroyer would be loading up another round of depth charges, but the U-571 should make it to the surface, first. All they needed was that damn torpedo, to put this boat back in the war.

From the voice tube came a report from the rear torpedo room: "Mr. Tyler! No go, sir."

"Tank," Tyler said stiffly into the intercom mike, " 'no go' is not acceptable."

"Trigger just can't reach it, sir!"

Tyler and Klough exchanged tight glances, then the U-571's only remaining captain ducked through the aft hatchway and ran full-throttle down the passageway until he entered the rear torpedo room, where the water had spilled up out of the open deck plates.

Tank had an arm around Trigger, who was soaked in filthy bilgewater from his matted hair to his sopping fatigues, coughing, leaning against the torpedo tube, miserable.

Tyler sloshed over to them. "What the hell is going on back here?"

Trigger shook his head, spoke between coughs. "Can't . . . can't get to it, sir. Can't . . . can't do it. . . . Arm's too short."

Tyler swallowed, and put a hand on the boy's shoulder. "Then you better grow, son, right now."

Tortured eyes looked out of the water-streaked baby face. "Sir . . . ?"

"We're going to be on the surface in about two minutes, got it? And we don't want to be up there staring down that Nazi tin can with no torpedo to say hello. You *have* to go back in there and try."

"But . . . but . . ."

"You're our only chance, Trigger. I wouldn't ask it of you, son, unless our lives depended on it. And they do."

Chest heaving, still trying to catch his breath, Trigger just looked at Tyler with an expression that said: *Ask me anything but to go back in that bilge.*

The boy shook his head. "No, sir. I'm sorry. I just can't do it."

Tyler took the sailor by his arm and dragged him, sloshed with him over to where the deck plates had been removed—the now underwater entrance to the bilge and all that filthy water and that maze of pipes.

"You can," Tyler said to the boy, locking eyes with him, "and you will. You are going to close that valve, sailor. Get in that bilge and do your job."

Trigger's expression hardened—it was part resolve, part rebuke; the eyes in the young face were suddenly old, and seemed to say to Tyler: *You do know you're killing me, don't you?*—and Trigger put the rebreather mouthpiece in, and affixed the nose clip (he would use them as long as he could), and hopped back down into the bilge.

The splash Trigger made had barely settled when Tyler, already hurrying forward, yelled back to Tank, "Report the instant that torpedo is ready to fire!"

As Tyler entered Control, the Chief said, "Thirty meters."

Tyler strode over to the hatchway near the hydrophone shack. "Talk to me, Mr. Wentz."

"Destroyer's under way, sir. Steady bearing. Closing on our position."

"Hell."

The Chief said, "Twenty meters. . . . Mr. Tyler?"

"Yes, Chief?"

Stepping away from his station, Klough circled as he spoke, taking in every face. "I'd just like to go on record saying this is the best goddamn crew I ever had the honor of servin' with, sir."

Tyler's eyes met Klough's; both men smiled, and nodded, just a little.

"Men," the Chief said, as he returned to his post, "whatever happens, know this: you've done yourselves, and the United States Navy, proud."

All eyes were on the Chief, and—perhaps embarrassed by his own speech—he returned his full attention to the depth meter, saying, "Ten meters, sir."

Tyler paced, muttering, "Come on, Trigger. Come on. You can do it. You can make it. . . ."

"Hold on!" the Chief yelled. "About to surface!"

Tyler, already at the periscope, said, "Raising 'scope," hitting the controls.

Then he was looking out at a calm, seemingly quiet sea, the destroyer not yet in his sights. Moments later, the U-571 broached the surface, with abrupt force, stirring waves, bow first, dropping down with a massive splash, jostling everyone on the boat, including Tyler at the 'scope.

In the bowels of the bilge, this sudden movement jarred Trigger, bouncing him between pipes, startling him more than hurting him. He no longer had the rebreather in—he was past that point—and was heading into the network of pipes and cables, that out-of-reach valve just ahead.

In the Control Room, Tyler had the destroyer in the periscope's viewscreen: seven hundred yards away, the warship was turning toward the U-571, trailing smoke, boilers at full blast.

"Got her," Tyler told his crew. "Heading straight for us. Helm, come right ten degrees."

"Right ten degrees," Rabbit said.

The Chief, reacting to a gauge, grabbed at the diving controls, saying, "Watch your planes, Eddie!"

Green, sweating, said, "Aye, Chief!"

Tyler said into the intercom mike, "Tank! Start the diesel, all ahead full!"

In the diesel room, Tank deftly operated valves, hitting the air starter—the diesel turned, caught hold, purring throatily to life. Tank engaged the clutch, raising the throttle till the rockers were a blur. Then, as he frantically checked that the engine was running properly, he hollered his report into the voice tube: "Port diesel ahead full, sir!"

In the Control Room, the destroyer in his periscope sights bearing down on them, Tyler said, "Good! Now get me a report on that torpedo tube!"

Every man in Control knew that, with the U-571 surfaced like this, without a torpedo, it was just a matter of time before the shells began.

And that time was now: the thunder of the destroyer's forward gun was followed by the shriek of the shell's flight and then it exploded, to the

U-571's portside, the impact shaking the ship and jarring every man aboard . . .

  . . . including Trigger, holding his breath underwater, weaving between pipes, which he was now slammed into with crushing force!

Then another shell made its banshee-cry journey, booming starboard.

The ship shuddered, and so did the crew.

In Tyler's periscope view, the destroyer was staring right at him. "Shit. Bastards got us bracketed." A puff of smoke told him another shell had been fired, before he even heard the initial boom. "Incoming!"

The shell exploded against the forward starboard side of the ship, with a deafening bellow that rocked the boat mercilessly. In the forward torpedo room, lockers flew open and an overwhelming exploding wall of water burst out.

"We're hit!" Eddie Green yelled. "Jesus, we're hit!"

And in the bilge beneath the rear torpedo room, Ted "Trigger" Fitzgerald had been tossed like a plaything, a heavy pipe toppling onto his back, pinning him there, underwater, against the iron floor, trapping him.

He struggled desperately to free himself, panic and air bubbling out of him—unable to reach that valve, so close, so far away, too busy drowning.

THE ROAR OF water assaulting his ears, Tyler bolted to the forward hatchway, where the sea was rolling in, and yelled out, "Wentz, get in here!" As the tidal wave threatened to engulf him, the radioman was clawing off the hydrophone headset, and Tyler reached in and yanked him away from his console, then, as Tyler tug-roped him through the hatch, Wentz dove into the Control Room.

At the same time, the Chief was shouting, "Eddie, get over there, help dog that hatch!"

Wentz had barely tumbled through when the mess steward was at Tyler's side, helping him shut that hatch against the high-pressure onslaught of flooding; Wentz got into the act, and then they had the damn thing shut, Green twisting the wheel, dogging it tight.

Wentz and Eddie just stood there, chests heaving, soaked to the bone; but the equally sopping Tyler was already halfway across the Control Room, snatching down the intercom mike. Through tight teeth, Tyler demanded, "Talk to me, Tank—what's that air gauge say?"

From the tube came Tank's agitated voice: "Sir! Still not ready, sir!"

"What the fuck next?" Tyler growled.

The muffled *boom*, *boom*, of the destroyer's deck guns provided the answer. The first shell missed, wide, but the second rocked the ship like nothing before, like those depth charges had been firecrackers, a thunderous explosion that all but shattered every eardrum on the U-571, a direct hit that blew the rear deck of the ship to flaming shards, knocking every damn one of them off their feet.

Down in the bilge of the rear torpedo room, way under the fireball rising from where the rear deck used to be, the enemy's big explosion had done the U-571 a small favor: the pipe trapping Ted "Trigger" Fitzgerald, a boy of seventeen who was within a minute of drowning, knocked loose, freeing him.

He didn't have much left, the "baby" of the old S-33; but somehow he wiggled forward and slipped his hand through the pipes and reached and reached and, finally, his fingers grasped that elusive valve.

Once he had hold of it, little strength was required to spin it shut—which was good, because little strength was what Trigger Fitzgerald had left in him.

In the Control Room, as the sound of flames snapped and cracked from down the aft passageway, the men were picking themselves up, and the Chief was saying, "Sir, request permission to abandon ship!"

Shaken, Tyler reached up to one of the periscope handles and hoisted himself up. He found himself looking into the hard eyes behind the wireframe glasses of Lieutenant Hirsch, who was just barely shaking his head, sending a grave message, which Tyler understood all too well.

"Chief," Tyler said, "we will leave this boat when we've finished our job."

And the Chief's eyes tightened; then—obviously aware that Tyler intended to go for broke—he nodded. The other crew members quickly gathered the implication, but no one said anything, except Eddie Green, who said, "Oh hell."

In the rear torpedo room, which no longer had a roof, smoke and sunshine streaming in, Tank crawled out from under a bunk, where he'd been hurled, and made his way to the air gauge, which still read negative.

"Poor kid," Tank muttered to himself.

And then the needle leapt forward.

Tyler was looking through the 'scope at the destroyer when Tank's voice blurted from the tube: "After torpedo tube ready in all respects, sir!"

Grinning at the 'scope, Tyler said, "Hold her right there, Rabbit. Fire! Shit—" He grabbed the intercom mike. "Fire! Fire! Now!" *Right now or we're dead in the water.*

And Tank—knowing Trigger was still down there in that maze of pipes, in that murky bilgewater world, either drowned or alive but too close to that tube to survive its firing—slammed the ball of his fist on the firing valve, sending pressurized water spraying out from the torpedo door's seal, followed by the satisfying *ka-thunk* of the fish firing perfectly out the stern tube, above the boat's twin rudders and screws, in a glorious burst of compressed air, courtesy of the late Ted "Trigger" Fitzgerald.

Tyler watched through the 'scope, as the torpedo screamed through the blue waters, trailing a blue-white frothy phosphorescent wake.

"Come on, baby," Tyler whispered, as if into the ear of a beautiful woman. "Baby, baby . . . come on. . . ."

It was running straight, hot and perfect, and Tyler allowed himself a smile, knowing, knowing he'd won, knowing the poor sons of bitches on the deck of that destroyer would be watching that torpedo cutting a line straight toward them, and there was nothing for them to do but use the last few seconds of their lives to pray, and to wait for the inevitable explosion as the torpedo sliced through the warship's hull like a knife through butter.

"Ka-boom," Tyler said softly.

Ka-BOOOOM! the destroyer echoed back, six hundred pounds of high explosives erupting under its keel, snapping the huge craft in half, like a twig.

Rearing back from the eyepiece, Tyler swallowed. Blinked. Looked again to see if he'd seen right.

But the men around him, who'd heard the world explode out there, knew they'd made a direct hit, and were cheering, as their captain said, quietly, "Yes."

He returned to the periscope and watched as the stern of the destroyer drove itself under the water, then as the bow floated, pointing straight up, like a drowning man extending a desperate hand . . . and sinking.

Tyler turned away from the 'scope, awestruck by the majesty of the destruction they'd wrought, and vaguely horrified. Pity for the men on that enemy ship flickered through him—sailors fighting for their country were dying in anguish, *right now*. It quickly passed, however—better them on the bottom, than these boys around him.

The cheers, too, had quickly passed, all that bottled up tension released at once: what Tyler noted around him were traded looks of amazement at still being alive, faces painted with relief, not triumph.

The Chief was at the periscope, seeing for himself. "Blew the bastard right in half."

"You said you wanted to put some Kraut tonnage on the bottom," Tyler reminded him.

Klough moved away from the periscope, grinning. "That I did . . . that I did. Mr. Tyler, permission to speak freely."

"Anything, Chief."

"You ever need a chief of the boat, Skipper, I'm ready to sign aboard with you any damn day."

Tyler smiled. "Thanks, Chief."

Hirsch extended a hand to him. "Pleasure to serve under you, Captain."

Tyler nodded, took the handclasp. "Mr. Hirsch, consider yourself a submariner."

An increased sound of nearby licking flames, aft, and rushing water, forward, prompted Tyler to grab the intercom mike, and yell, "Tank! Tank, get your ass up here! Tank, are you all right?"

"N-no, sir." Tank's voice came not from the tube, but from the hatchway, where he leaned, smudged with soot, streaked with grease. All eyes turned his way.

Tyler winced. "Trigger . . . ?"

He shook his head, glumly. "Didn't make it, sir. 'Fraid he drowned down there, or else bought it when we fired the fish."

Hirsch stood with head lowered. Eddie Green began to pray. The Chief crossed himself. Wentz slumped and sat at the chart table. Rabbit, still seated at the planes, began to quietly weep.

And Tank just stared at Tyler—hard—a look that was part regret, part accusation.

"That boy saved our lives," Tyler said.

Tank gulped, nodded. Nods all around.

Then Eddie Green said, "You and Trigger did, Captain. Two of you together saved us."

Looking from face to face, Tyler was amazed to see these men nodding—even Rabbit. And Tank.

The ship expressed its own opinion, with a sudden shuddering and an ungodly groan that sounded like the death rattle of a great beast.

"Skipper," the Chief said, "I'm good, but even God Almighty couldn't keep this tub afloat much longer."

"Okay, Chief," Tyler said. "Permission to abandon ship. In other words, let's get the hell off of this Nazi scow."

This elicited a positive response, to say the least, and as Hirsch withdrew the Enigma machine from under the chart table, Tyler had one last look at the Control Room of his first command, then followed his men up the conning tower ladder.

Soon the crew of the U-571—with a canvas bag

packed with the Enigma machine and emergency
provisions—were afloat in an inflatable German
raft on an ocean turned orange by flames. They
paddled away from the U-boat, watching as water
streamed out from the edges of the torpedo hatch,
their ears filled with a terrible metallic wail, wide
eyes witnessing that hatch burst open and a geyser
of seawater cascade out.

When the U-571 began to sink by its stern, the
men in the life raft—every one of them—felt a
strange pang, though no one said anything. They
were, of course, remembering their fallen friends—
Lars, whose widow would grieve; Dahlgren, who
left a wife and young daughter; Pete Emmett,
whose magic had run out; Major Coonan, the combat expert killed so early; Griggs, who died before
Tyler's eyes; Mazzola, the lover who went out
fighting; Trigger, who had given his life for
theirs. . . .

Yet that odd sensation, this peculiar tug of emotion, was out of more than just mourning those
who'd lost their lives on this mission. No one
wanted to admit that this Nazi submarine had been,
for a time, for a *key* time in their lives as men and
as sailors, their ship, their boat, their home, their
means of attacking the enemy and serving their
country.

And none of them seemed surprised—and no
one commented at all—when Lieutenant Andrew
J. Tyler saluted, just before the ship slipped under.

Before long, the ocean was again painted orange,
not by flames this time—both the U-571 and the
destroyer *Anschluss* were long since on the ocean's

floor—but by the setting sun, the inflatable a mere yellow dot in these vast shimmering waters.

Tyler did not know what fate awaited him, and his men—death by exhaustion and dehydration possibly, maybe plucked from the sea for imprisonment by the Germans (the Enigma pitched overboard), or perhaps they would wash ashore, as they hoped, as they intended, at Land's End.

Whatever lay ahead, Tyler knew only that they would face it together, as a crew, under their captain's watch.

A Tip of the Captain's Cap

Several acknowledgments are necessary, starting with Jonathan Mostow, whose lively script provided the basis for this novel; Mr. Mostow really did his homework, for which I am grateful. The needs of a novel and a screenplay are different, of course, and for that reason, I consulted a number of books on submarining; I take all responsibility for inaccuracies, however, and neither Mr. Mostow nor the authors of the books that follow should shoulder any blame—and I defer in advance to those in my audience whose expertise in this area exceeds mine.

Four books in particular provided background for this novel: *Battle Below: The War of the Submarines* (1945) by Robert J. Casey; *Silent Running: My Years on a World War II Attack Submarine* (1995) by James F. Calvert, Vice Admiral, USN (ret.); *Iron Coffins* (1969) by Herbert A. Werner; and *U-Boat War* (1978) by Lothar-Gunther Buchheim (whose war experiences were the basis for director Wolfgang Petersen's 1981 film, *Das Boot*). The first two of these gave me the American view of the "silent service" (a term World War II sub-

242

mariners seemed to despise) and the latter pair provided the German perspective.

Other books consulted include: *The Battle for the Atlantic: World War II* (1977) by Barrie Pitt and the editors of Time-Life Books; *Submarines: The History and Evolution of Underwater Fighting Vessels* (1975) by Anthony Preston; *The Underwater War 1939–1945* (1982) by Commander Richard Compton-Hall, MBE, RN (ret.); and the New Hampshire WPA Guide (1938).

I would also like to thank Joe Collins (no relation), who provided his usual expertise on military and weapons matters; my father, Max A. Collins, Sr., a naval ensign in World War II, who offered insights and information; Cindy Chang of Universal Studios, who provided her typical, amazingly prompt support; my editor, Tia Maggini; my agent Dominick Abel; and my wife, Barbara Collins, who always helps keep the boat afloat.

MAX ALLAN COLLINS has earned an unprecedented nine Private Eye Writers of America Shamus nominations for his Nathan Heller historical thrillers, winning twice (*True Detective*, 1983, and *Stolen Away*, 1991).

A Mystery Writers of America Edgar nominee in both fiction and nonfiction categories, Collins has been hailed as "the Renaissance man of mystery fiction." His credits include five suspense novel series, film criticism, songwriting, trading-card sets and movie tie-in novels, including such international bestsellers as *In the Line of Fire*, *The Mummy*, *Air Force One*, *Saving Private Ryan* and *Mommy* (from his own film), which was chosen as one of the Ten Best Horror Novels of 1997 by Barnes and Noble.

He scripted the internationally syndicated comic strip *Dick Tracy* from 1977 to 1993, is co-creator of the comic-book features *Ms. Tree, Wild Dog* and *Mike Danger*, and has written the *Batman* comic book and newspaper strip.

Working as an independent filmmaker in his native Iowa, he wrote, directed and produced the

cult-favorite suspense film *Mommy*, starring
Patty McCormack, and performed the same du-
ties for a well-received sequel, *Mommy's Day*.
He also wrote the HBO World Premiere film,
The Expert, and wrote and directed the award-
winning documentary, *Mike Hammer's Mickey
Spillane*.

Collins lives in Muscatine, Iowa, with his
wife, writer Barbara Collins, and their teenage
son, Nathan.